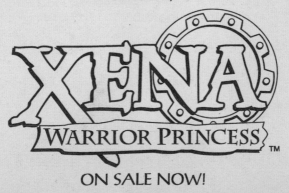

HERCULES
THE LEGENDARY JOURNEYS™

SERPENT'S SHADOW

A novel by Timothy Boggs
based on the Universal television series
created by Christian Williams

BOULEVARD BOOKS, NEW YORK

HERCULES: THE LEGENDARY JOURNEYS:
SERPENT'S SHADOW

A novel by Timothy Boggs, based on the Universal television series
HERCULES: THE LEGENDARY JOURNEYS, created by
Christian Williams

A Boulevard Book/published by arrangement with
MCA Publishing Rights, a Division of MCA, Inc.

PRINTING HISTORY
Boulevard edition/December 1996

The Putnam Berkley World Wide Web site address is
http://www.berkley.com/berkley

Make sure to check out *PB Plug*, the science fiction/fantasy newsletter, at
http://www.pbplug.com

ISBN: 1-57297-214-9

BOULEVARD
Boulevard Books are published by The Berkley Publishing Group,
200 Madison Avenue, New York, New York 10016.
BOULEVARD and its logo are trademarks
belonging to Berkley Publishing Corporation.

PRINTED IN THE UNITED STATES OF AMERICA

10   9   8   7   6   5   4   3   2   1

For my brothers:
Lionel Fenn, Simon Lake, and Geoffrey Marsh.
Thanks, gentlemen, for bringing me up right.

And for Barry Neville, super editor,
lover of Killer Klowns,
and the man who undid all my brothers' work,
bless his little heart.

SERPENT'S SHADOW

1

For a while, near sunset, it seemed as if the gulls had taken over the world.

They swarmed over the sea, sometimes diving, sometimes coming up with flashes of silver wriggling in their beaks; they clouded over the fishing boats heading back to shore, complaining loudly, swooping, trying to snatch fishes from a net on a fishing boat; they sat like white-haired old men on the high massive boulders at the north end of the harbor, watching the other birds, one leg tucked up, never making a sound, the steady sea breeze puffing their feathers.

For Holix, the sight never failed to please, even though he had seen it a thousand times. Coasting on the thermals, gliding on the breeze, confident that sooner or later they would get what they wanted, the birds fascinated him.

Whenever he was able to escape from the training stables, he came here to watch them. He loved sitting high above the beach, at the edge of the plain on a favorite flat-topped boulder the sea never reached except in the fiercest of storms. Directly below, the other rocks sloped down to the water. Jagged and tall inland, they grew shorter as they approached the surf, seeming to do battle with the waves.

Like the teeth of a dragon, he thought; ready to snap shut and crush the first human who passed by.

He scowled, and scolded himself for thinking such a gruesome thought.

Yet he couldn't help it.

Something was out there.

Everyone knew it, but no one wanted to talk about it. And when you asked, they either yelled, or aimed a kick to drive you away, or simply pretended they hadn't understood.

But *something* was out there.

He was determined to find out what it was.

He shifted to ease the stiffness in his rump, grinning when one of the rock-sitting gulls glared up at him, fluffed its feathers, and looked away disdainfully.

"I could have you for dinner," he said lightly.

The gull ignored him.

"Hey," a voice said behind him. "He's talking to the birds again."

The sound of giggling made him turn, a mock scowl on his face.

There were three of them on the grass, passing around a wineskin and a basket of fresh bread. From the way they tried and failed to sit straight, and the sight of the flattened wineskin tossed on the ground, it was clear that they had already begun the party.

Not that he really minded. Jax, who worked with an armorer, had been the first to befriend him when he had arrived; and the twins, Sana and Cire, had decided he would be the brother they'd always wished they had.

Like he really wanted to be their *brother*.

Cire, lush red hair and a figure that had more curves than the coastline, beckoned him away from the rock. "We're supposed to be having fun, Holix," she said with a pout.

"Not being glum and brooding," finished Sana.

At least he thought it was Sana. He was pretty sure it was Sana. Even after all these months, he could barely tell them apart.

Jax, tall and lanky, his black hair in tight curls around his head, tossed him the wineskin. "He's not being glum, he's contemplating great thoughts. Figuring out the workings of the world."

"Oh, not that again," Sana complained. "Pass the wine."

Cire pointed to the horizon. "There's nothing out there but water, Holix. Deep water. Lots of deep water."

"And fish," Sana added.

"Okay, and fish."

"But nothing else."

"Of course not. Except for the boats."

"Well, sure, the boats. And the birds."

"Absolutely."

Holix blinked and looked to Jax, who only shrugged and tore off some bread, shoved it in his mouth, and grinned around the crumbs as he chewed.

"It's the festival," Sana decided with a knowing nod.

"Right," her twin agreed.

"It can get very confusing."

"Of course it can."

Holix filled his mouth with wine, swallowed, coughed, and handed the skin back to Jax.

"So much to do," Sana said—unless it was Cire.

"So little time."

"Exciting, though."

"And scary."

"Oh, not really. Not if you know what's going on."

"Well, that's true."

"Of course, even if you know what's going on, it can be kind of scary. In an exciting sort of way."

Cire giggled—unless it was Sana.

I'm getting dizzy, Holix thought, and looked over their heads to the trees some fifty feet away. They were tall and slender, slightly bent from the constant breeze, with silvery-green foliage that fluttered and whispered. They formed a single line a hundred yards long east to west along the heights above the beach, and some of the leaves winked hints of gold as the sun continued its glide toward the horizon.

"Do we have to talk about this?" Jax complained. "After tonight, we're barely going to have time to breathe."

Holix agreed. He had been in the city less than a year, and while it had been a wonderful experience

4

up to now, it was threatening to turn into something else entirely. For the next several weeks he and the other stable hands would have to practice braiding the horses' tails and manes, entwining them with silk ribbons and gold tassels. Perfect, his boss had said; everything had to be perfect, or the gods would be displeased.

He would also have to ride the animals, alone, because of his experience. Training them to march, to high-step, to pull chariots, to keep their calm amid throngs of cheering people would consume his every waking moment, and probably some sleeping ones as well. Tonight, then, would undoubtedly be the last opportunity for the four of them to have any peace for months. Or any substantial time together.

Sighing silently, he looked back at the sea. The setting sun to his left had nearly touched the water; a half mile along the beach to his right the last of the fishing boats were coasting toward their piers.

The gulls were in full flight.

Far beyond the breakers a single boat worked one last catch before nightfall.

Holix wondered what it was like out there.

"There he goes again," Jax said, a hint of friendly laughter in his voice.

Throwing the nets, hauling in the fish, riding the swells that never stopped.

"I think it's cute."

Cire, he realized; that was Cire. Her voice was husky; Sana's was smooth.

She thinks it's cute.

5

He rolled his eyes. Cute is not what I want to be. Cute is a puppy or a kitten. Or a brother. I want to be—

"It's not cute, it's morbid," Sana said.

"No, it's not," he answered without turning around. "I just want to know things, that's all. And one of the things I want to know is, what happens to the queen of the festival after everything's over?"

No one answered.

The sun cast a streak of fire across the surface of the sea, catching the lone fishing boat and turning it into a flimsy silhouette against the darkening sky.

"They move on," Jax suggested finally, although he didn't sound very certain. "Something as important as that, they don't want to stay around here. They want to see the world."

"Why? It's beautiful here. It's . . . perfect."

"Spoken like a true farmer," Sana said flatly.

Holix didn't look; he didn't respond. Besides, he hadn't really been a farmer. He had grown up on his family's farm, true, but it had been discovered early on that he had a special talent for training animals, especially horses. So that's what he did now, and that's why he had been picked by the stable master to help train the festival horses.

And that's when he realized with a start why the twins' master and mistress had been spending so much time around the council chambers lately—they wanted one of the girls to be summer queen. The honor that would bring to the household would be incalculable.

You know, he thought, sometimes you can be thick as a post, Holix, you jerk.

"Look," Jax said to Sana, "if you're going to be like that, we're not going to have any fun at all."

"He's right." Cire was taking someone else's side for a change.

Holix heard Sana mumble something that had the tone of an apology, but he didn't turn around. With one hand shielding his face from the final glare of the sun, he stared at the fishing boat.

Despite the distance, he could tell something was wrong.

"Hey," he said quietly.

The sea was calm, but the little craft had begun to rock alarmingly.

"Quit hogging the wine," Cire complained lightly.

"I'm not hogging, I'm . . . tasting," Jax insisted.

"You're drunk," said Sana in disgust. And hiccuped.

Cire giggled. And hiccuped.

"Hey," Holix said, louder.

"Ladies, ladies," Jax called out grandly. "There's plenty for everyone." He belched and groaned.

"Disgusting," Cire said.

"Very," Sana agreed.

There was very little light now, but Holix, squinting and leaning forward, could have sworn he saw something more in the dark out there, something that wasn't part of the boat.

"Hey!"

"What now?" Sana snapped.

7

He pointed as he turned to them. "Look!"

Cire, who seemed to have caught his alarm, crawled quickly to his side, her shoulder touching his. "What, Holix?"

"There," he said. "See out there?"

She raised a hand to cut the wind from her eyes, and shook her head. "I don't see anything."

Slowly Holix lowered his arm.

She was right.

The boat was gone.

It should have been a perfect moment, a dream moment. Cire beside him, the tickling of her breeze-touched hair against his cheek, the feel of her shoulder against his, the smell of her skin . . . it should have been perfect.

But the boat was gone.

And *something* was out there.

2

The wall was not nearly finished, but the man who was building it was in no real hurry. It would be nice when it was done, the protection it offered complete, but the digging, the hauling, the fitting of the stones, all this gave him a chance to be alone, to think without distraction, to let his mind wander and dream of things that might have been, or that might yet be.

This particular section reached just to his thighs, and while it wasn't high enough yet, it suited him for now. He didn't have to bend over so far, and the lifting was still quite easy. Another advantage—he didn't have far to sink when he wanted to sit down.

A large rock balanced on the broad top, bridging a gap. He closed one eye and tilted his head, measuring. When he was sure he was right, he raised a hand over his head, stared at the rock, and slowed his breathing. Concentrated. Pushed up on his toes, and suddenly brought his arm down more swiftly than lightning.

The side of his hand struck the rock squarely, sparks darted into the afternoon sunlight, and the rock split.

9

The larger portion fell neatly into the gap; the smaller flew into the trees on the other side of the wall.

He grinned his satisfaction, looked around to see if anyone had observed him, then grimaced, sagged a little, grabbed his wrist with his free hand, and groaned, "Damn, but that hurts."

"I heard that," a woman's voice sang.

Great, he thought; great.

"Sorry, Mother."

A woman stepped out of the trees behind him, a basket of fresh flowers tucked under one arm. She was slender and fair-haired, with hints of gray that appeared only when the light touched her head a certain way. Her face was slightly rounded and unlined, with flushed cheeks and a sheen of perspiration across her high brow.

"You know, you could use a hammer like ordinary people, Hercules," she scolded with a smile.

Hercules smiled back. "That would be too easy." He leaned over and stuck his hand into a wood bucket filled with water. He sighed, exaggerating his relief so she would laugh aloud.

She did.

"You look warm," he said when the stinging finally stopped. "Sit for a while."

Even as the protest began to form on her lips his hands were around her waist and she was up and seated on the wall.

"Well," she said, setting the basket beside her and smoothing her dress primly. "Showing off again?"

"Since when do I have to show off for you?"

He sat at her feet, his back to her legs, knees up

10

and hands clasped loosely around his shins, grateful for the opportunity to take a break, half closing his eyes when he felt her hand brush across his hair.

They remained silent for several minutes, listening to the birdsong in the woods, the drone of bees in the meadow, the almost inaudible whisper of a fitful breeze in the branches.

"You realize, of course," said Alcmena quietly, "that you're driving me crazy."

He frowned. "What are you talking about? Don't you like me to come around?"

Her hand slapped the top of his head lightly. "Of course I do, you know that. I don't see you often enough."

"Then what's the problem?"

She gestured left and right. "The wall."

He remembered her original reaction to his project—that she didn't need a wall to protect the house and land—and his response, which was that she shouldn't refuse the protection it would offer, not when she lived alone.

Not having to add that it would make him feel a lot better to know she was secure while he was away.

"What about it?"

"Stop pouting. It doesn't become you." She cuffed him again.

"I'm not," he complained, even as he heard the pout in his voice. He laughed easily, and tilted his head back to butt her legs gently. "Okay. I am. But what about the wall? I thought you decided it was all right."

"It is, Hercules," she said patiently. "It is. But whenever you come home, you work on it a little, sit with me a lot, we talk, we go into the village, and the days pass.'' A pause that held a silent sigh. ''Too quickly sometimes. Too quickly.''

''So?''

''Hush.'' Another cuff. ''So sooner or later you're out here most of the day—''

''Mother—''

''—thinking.''

Immediately, he realized the truth of her words, and lowered his head. ''I'm sorry. I didn't—''

Her voice was tender. ''Hercules, you're my son. I know you too well. Either you have a problem you won't tell me about, or you're getting restless.'' Melancholy replaced the tenderness. ''You're getting ready to move on.''

He twisted around so he could look up at her face. ''You're right.''

''I know.''

''I hate it when you're right.''

''I know that, too.''

He squeezed her ankle. ''Sort of.''

Her eyebrow lifted. ''Sort of?''

''I'm not really restless, and I don't have a problem.'' He stared at the grass at the base of the wall. ''This time it's just a feeling. I don't know. A premonition, maybe.''

She waggled her fingers, a signal to let her climb down. When he complied, they strolled through the sparse woods toward her house. The shade was cool, the sun warm, and wildflowers grew in profusion here and in the meadow after two days of light but steady rain.

"You're worried about Hera," she said.

He was about to contradict her when, abruptly, he realized that, once again and maddeningly, she was right. Yet it wasn't precisely worry. It was more like anticipation. It had been so long since his vindictive stepmother had tried to kill him that it was making him nervous. Unless, of course, that was the reason why she was waiting so long to try to kill him again—to make him nervous. In which case, he ought to become more alert, not more ill at ease. Unless, of course, making him ill at ease was the reason why she was waiting so long to try again to kill him. . . .

Alcmena laughed softly and hooked her hand around his arm. "Don't think about it so much. You'll make yourself dizzy."

"Too late," he muttered as they stepped out of the trees.

The house was modest, appearing smaller than it was because of the trees that rose about it, protecting it from winds hot and cold, and from sun and storms. In a garden that was set to one side, Alcmena grew her own vegetables, as well as flowers whose exotic beauty rivaled those developed by the professionals around Corinth and Sparta.

A place of comfort.

A place of serenity.

As they approached the entrance Alcmena grunted softly and nudged him toward a long and low marble bench near the garden. "You go sit. I'll have Pleophy fetch you when dinner's ready."

"What?" He feigned insult. "Don't you want me to cook tonight?"

13

"Sit," she ordered, and waited until he did. "You cooked last night, as I remember."

So he had, and the memory made him wince. So did the words Pleophy, his mother's handmaiden, used when she had seen the fruits of his labor in the kitchen. A young woman, he had thought, shouldn't know words that only soldiers used.

He surrendered with an apologetic smile. "All right. I'll wait."

Alcmena leaned over and kissed his brow. "And stop worrying about Hera. She'll do what she does when she does it. No sooner. Your fretting isn't going to rush her." She kissed him again and went inside, but not before he caught the concern in her eyes.

She knew full well that Hera would not rest until he was with Hades; she also knew that he would not rest until, somehow, he had exacted full revenge on the goddess who had murdered his wife and three children.

A revenge that would take him the rest of his life to accomplish.

Even then it would not be enough to repay the goddess for her crimes.

All right, all right, he scolded himself harshly; that's enough. You're home, and Mother doesn't need this burden.

That was certainly the truth. Every time he arrived, she nearly wept with joy at the sight of him, and with relief that he was still alive; and every time he left, she did her best to hide her fears and the tears they caused her to shed. She also did her best to live a normal life during his absences, but he understood

14

from his friends in the village that she worried constantly.

He knew from listening to her talk that she was aware of what he was doing most of the time, because Zeus, his father, made it a point to inform her about his welfare.

That should have been comforting.

It wasn't; not really.

He hadn't spoken to his father since his family had been taken from him, because Zeus had been too busy with a woman either to stop Hera from the killing or to warn Hercules' family about her plans. Alcmena had told him more than once that Zeus was heartbroken and shamed by Hera's acts. But Hercules didn't care. Zeus couldn't possibly be as heartbroken as he, and he doubted his father even knew what real shame was.

He had loved his father once.

Perhaps he still did, but that love was clouded now with something very close to hate.

Hercules stared at the flowers, teeth clenched, hands folded into fists, until he realized what he was doing. He closed his eyes briefly, opened them, and this time *saw* the flowers, with their vivid blossoms, and smelled their soothing scent. He breathed deeply and relaxed.

Wondering if maybe it wasn't time to get back on the road.

Let the cycle begin anew.

Or maybe there was still time before dinner to work a little on the wall.

He stood.

He looked at the house.

He looked past the house to the empty road.

He felt a twinge in his hand and checked it, shaking his head at the bruise and the slight swelling. Oh sure, he thought; don't use a hammer, chop it with your bare hand. Bloody show-off.

He examined the hand again.

Bloody show-off, in more ways than one.

A moment later he heard someone singing boisterously, and saw a figure striding jauntily up the road, pack slung over one shoulder, left hand on a scabbard at his hip.

"Mother," he called, "we're having company for dinner."

He heard her response, and sat again, straddling the bench. Waiting. Hoping against hope that the singing would soon stop. He had heard sows with better voices, and they weren't even trying to sing.

The figure waved as it vanished behind the house.

Hercules sensed someone watching. When he turned, he saw Alcmena in the arched doorway, leaning a little too casually against the wall. He shook his head. "You knew?"

She shrugged one shoulder. "I had a feeling." She grinned. "Just like you." And she was gone again.

Seconds later Iolaus bounded around the corner of the house, dropped his pack, and sat opposite him.

"You're looking well, Hercules."

"You don't look so bad yourself."

Iolaus was a full head shorter than Hercules, his hair wavy and long and touched by the sun. He didn't look all that strong, but he was; he did appear quick and agile, and he was. Although he could wield the

16

sword, and the dagger tucked in his belt, like Hercules he preferred a good thumping to a killing.

After a moment's silence he rubbed his hands briskly. "I was just passing through, thought I'd stop by to check on your mother."

"Sure you were."

"A wonderful coincidence, don't you think?"

"Sure it is."

Iolaus leaned away. "Hercules," he said, sounding indignant. "Hercules, don't you believe me?"

Hercules smiled. "Should I?"

His best friend shook his head sadly. "I don't understand. A man comes to visit, and all he gets is suspicion."

"Suspicion? You haven't even said hello yet."

"Oh." Iolaus offered his hand. "Hello."

"Hello yourself." Hercules took the hand, shook it, then suddenly yanked Iolaus into a back-pounding embrace that soon had them both laughing. When they sobered, he said, "So tell me all about this coincidence, Iolaus."

"There. See? Suspicion."

"No," he said. "I just know you, that's all."

"I'm hurt."

"You're a fraud."

"Okay. But I'm still hurt."

Hercules laughed once, quickly, and watched as Iolaus gathered his pack onto the bench and rooted through it.

"Wait until you see this, Herc. It's amazing. It's the most amazing thing I've ever seen in my life. You'll love it. You'll just love it."

"No."

On the bench between them Iolaus piled some clothes, flint, wrapped food that smelled as if it should have been buried three days ago, more clothes, a whetstone for his blades, and some things Hercules decided instantly he didn't want to learn more about.

"I know it's here," Iolaus muttered. "I saw it yesterday."

"What?"

"You'll see."

"Iolaus, I'll be dead of old age by the time you find what you're looking for."

Iolaus waved a hand. "Nah. You'll—aha!" He held up a small object triumphantly. "Here it is!"

Hercules looked at it. "It's a scroll."

"Exactly!"

"I've seen them before. They have writing on them."

"Exactly!"

As much as Hercules loved his friend, there were times, like now, when he wanted to whack him around a little, just to see if somehow that might force him to make more sense. A futile and an admittedly not very serious hope.

Iolaus slapped the scroll into Hercules' palm. "It's an invitation."

"To what?"

"Hercules," Iolaus announced solemnly, "it is an invitation to the greatest event in the history of my life. Your life. Our lives. This, Hercules, is going to make us rich!"

Hercules said nothing.

18

"All right," Iolaus admitted, "maybe it won't make us rich. But it'll sure make us famous."

Hercules looked toward the house, hoping someone would call them to dinner. Now.

"Well, maybe not famous, either." Iolaus tapped the scroll with one finger, then shifted the finger to Hercules' chest. "But it will make us popular, my friend."

"I don't get it. How will this—"

Iolaus smiled broadly. "Women, Herc. Popular with women. Beautiful, sensuous, available, eager, stunning, magnificent, stupendous women!"

"How?" was all Hercules said.

Iolaus puffed out his chest. "By being the judges of a beauty contest, that's how."

Give him one more chance, Hercules thought; then you can whack him.

"What beauty contest?"

Iolaus sighed. "Aren't you paying attention?" He waved the scroll in Hercules' face. "This one. And I'll tell you this—it's one thing we can do together that won't nearly get us killed."

Well, if that's true, Hercules thought, it would be a first.

But as they headed for the house he paused, frowned, and looked back and up.

A few wisps of cloud, a flock of dark birds, nothing more.

So why did he have the feeling something was up there, something watching?

Something waiting.

3

Themon did not always sit on the bountiful plain its residents now called home. Originally it was right off the beach, a comfortable mixture of farmers, herders, and fishermen. But the farmers, the herders, and most of the fishermen quickly grew tired of rebuilding their homes every time a storm drove in from the sea, raising the tides and flattening everything in sight, as well as a few things they didn't even realize had been there in the first place.

They considered it a sign.

Within a single year the entire population, except for a few hardheaded fishermen, had moved inland, and the new village they built soon grew to a town that quickly burgeoned into a small city. The mile ride to the beach and harbor was a small price to pay for not having to wake up one morning to find your bed transformed into a raft. And not a very stable one, at that.

In Themon, swimming wasn't a sport, it was a matter of survival.

In the city's center was a magnificent plaza, tiled in marble and lined with marble columns that lofted statues of the gods above the surrounding rooftops. Reaching southward from the plaza was a wide boulevard made smooth by interlocking paving stones, lined with busy shops and dining establishments. All the other north-south streets were paved as well, but only the boulevard extended beyond the city's boundary and ran all the way to where the grassy plain sloped sharply downward to the sand.

The council that ran the city was housed in an impressive two-story structure at the north side of the plaza. Eight steps took the visitor to a wide porch inlaid with turquoise and crimson tiles and lined with columns almost as impressive as those that lined the plaza. Beneath an overhanging peaked roof was a set of double doors paneled in bronze. Past the doors was a long corridor lit by torchlight at night, and by the sun in daylight because of a rectangular hole in the roof.

At the end of the corridor was another set of double doors, these ornamented with silver and gold medallions. Beyond this threshold was the council chamber, where laws were set, judgments rendered, and citizens either honored or disgraced.

There were nine men on the council, elected every five years.

The head of the council was Titus Perical.

In fact, Titus had been leader for so long, there were few who remembered who had preceded him in the office.

Titus hated the chamber. It was chilly and drafty,

it echoed every word and sneeze, it had truly dreadful artwork and statuary, and every time it rained, water ran down the central corridor and under the double doors with the silver and gold inlays, as if to remind the council that the sea might be distant but the rain could ruin a good set of sandals just as easily as a wave.

He had been trying for over a decade to hire someone to cover the roof. Tradition, however, foiled him every time.

It wasn't tradition, though, that brought him to a narrow, winding tunnel carved out of the cliff face on the west end of the harbor. The boulders that reached into the sea protected the secret entrance. Getting to that entrance meant using the beach, or climbing down from the cliff's edge.

Titus was not a climber.

At the end of the tunnel was a chamber wide enough to hold four men and high enough for one tall man to stand on the shoulders of another.

In this chamber there were no representations of Demeter or Poseidon, no offerings to Zeus or Aphrodite, no luxuries at all.

There was a simple stone bench that faced an arched niche in which had been set a simple altar made of dark brown stone. Flanking the niche were two ordinary stone pedestals upon which had been placed two ordinary candlesticks.

Carved out of the black stone wall behind the altar were two large green eyes. Slanted at the corners. Not at all human, and yet too human looking to belong to a beast.

Titus sat on the bench, his plain robes gathered around him as if he were cold.

On the altar was the beheaded body of a small deer, whose blood ran along four trenches in the stone, each ending at one corner. On the ground beneath each corner was a gold bowl into which the blood ran. Drop by drop.

"It's getting harder," Titus said wearily. His head was bowed, but he could feel those eyes staring at him. "Very hard."

He waited a moment.

The only sound was the deafening bellow of the sea.

He never questioned why the tide never reached here, why the waves had never found their way inside.

"I'm not complaining, you understand," he added hastily. "I know what has to done. It's just that . . . well, it's very hard these days. You know how *they* are. They have no respect for tradition. All they want to do is party, have a good time, and expect us to catch them when they fall." He shook his head in sorrow for the good old days. "Used to be, they *wanted* to grow up to be the queen. Used to be . . ." He sighed, and smiled at the memory. "Used to be they'd sooner kill whoever they thought might be their competition than lose. They had more spunk then. More ambition."

He squirmed; the damn bench was hard, and his butt was getting sore. "It's not like that now."

The sea thundered.

A voice said, "This will be the last time."

Titus started and nearly slid off the bench. "What? The last time?"

"Yes."

The voice was calm and quiet, yet not even the roar of the sea could smother it.

"The last time."

Titus wasn't sure how he felt about this news. For his entire life the festival had been the lifeblood of the city, had spurred its inhabitants to create bigger and better things, larger buildings, more contacts with other cities and towns, not to mention voyages across the sea to places that most never heard of.

On the other hand, the end of the festival would mean that he and his family would finally be free of the curse that made him a slave to this—

"The festival will go on."

He frowned. "But—"

"The other. That will end with this year."

"Ah." He understood. He thought he understood. He certainly hoped he understood, because he had no intention of being chomped in the middle of the night just because he got something wrong. "Ah."

Waves, split by the boulders, slammed against the cliff wall, and the chamber trembled. Clouds of loose dirt swirled down from the ceiling.

"But only," the voice continued, "if you do what you are told."

Titus drew himself up and faced the eyes squarely. "Have I ever failed you? Ever?"

A moment. Then: "No."

"Then I won't fail you now," Titus said.

And thought: what choice do I have?

"You sound very sure of yourself, Titus Perical."

He wasn't, but he was sure glad he sounded that way.

"I am."

"And what about the rebels?"

He laughed without making a sound, and his expression hardened, his voice growing harsh. "Rebels? They're not rebels, they're pests. They're not smart enough to try anything more than painting words on the walls, and their numbers are not large enough to frighten a newborn child." He spat dryly to one side. "Rebels. I have been Council Head longer than most of them have been alive. They will be no trouble. No trouble at all."

"Will there be blood?"

He shrugged. "There's always blood." He certainly hoped there wouldn't be, but since that's what the voice expected him to say, he said it.

The chamber walls shook again, mildly.

The voice boomed, "And have you heard?"

"They're coming," he answered. "I've had word already."

"Good."

"I expect they'll be here in a couple of days."

"Wonderful."

He allowed himself a self-congratulatory smile, but not so big that he would make himself a target. You could never tell with the gods and their capricious ways. One day they were all friendly and kind and showing you how to make a dinar or two that wasn't exactly legal; the next, they were threatening you with earthquakes and pestilence and lopping your legs off

25

so you had to crawl to Hades and hope he didn't turn you into a football.

Titus waited until there was a lull in the sea's thunder.

"There's . . . if you don't mind, of course . . . there's one thing I'd like to know."

"Yes?"

"What about, uh . . . you know. Klothon."

The voice sounded impatient: "Klothon will do what Klothon always does."

"Of course, of course, naturally." Titus hunched his shoulders, and ducked his head again. "It's just that, well, if the . . ." He almost choked, and ordered himself not to break down now. The meeting was almost over. "If the sacrifice isn't going to be—"

"Klothon," the voice repeated, with a faint hint of annoyance, "will do what Klothon always does."

That was another problem with the gods. They were always repeating the same thing over and over again, as if he hadn't heard the first time.

He nodded thoughtfully. "I see."

There was no response.

"So, if Klothon will do what Klothon always does, I guess I'll have to figure out a way to make sure it's done someplace else next time he's around."

There was no response.

Thinking the meeting had gone quite well so far, all in all, Titus dared to ask, "I don't suppose you'd like to give me a hint on how I'm supposed to pull that off?"

The chamber shook.

Clots of dirt showered from the ceiling.

The candles were caught in a wind he could not

feel, and their flames expanded, brightened to a glaring white, and vanished.

From the place on the floor where he had unceremoniously landed after sliding off the bench, Titus said, "No. I guess you're not going to tell me how to pull it off."

Yet he waited another hour, praying silently, just in case there were more instructions. When it was evident that the meeting was over, he picked up a sack and removed four gold lids from it. He placed one lid over each bowl, fastened them shut, and put the bowls into the sack.

Now there was no light.

He didn't need it.

When he was ready, he bowed out of the chamber and made his way along the tunnel toward the beach. He didn't concern himself with the deer's body. It would be gone when he returned, as it had been in the past, and he had never wanted to know how. Or why.

Or, for that matter, what.

Salt spray dampened his face as he neared the end of the passageway. He had taken too long; the tide was already flooding in.

Wonderful, he thought; I'm going to get drenched, I'm going to ruin my new sandals, and I still haven't figured out who's going to die next week.

He sighed for the burdens his office placed on his shoulders, sighed for the first wave that splashed him to the knees, and would have sighed for the new task he had been given had he not spotted the women on the beach.

Lovely women.

Extraordinary women.

Young women.

A brief glance at the sky in thanks, and he strode confidently toward them. And the closer he got, the more he smiled.

Perfect; they were absolutely perfect.

All he needed was the right speech, perhaps a bauble or two, and they were his. All his.

Another glance at the sky—and all yours, of course, he added silently. And all yours.

That the judges might not agree concerned him not in the least. At other festivals all it took to convince anyone to go along with him was a pouch filled with jewels or gold coin, or a whispered word to the wise that he knew what the judge in question had really been up to when he was last in Athens, allegedly at a goldsmith seminar.

This year none of that would be necessary.

This year neither of the judges would live long enough to utter any complaints.

4

"No," Hercules insisted firmly. "Absolutely not. It's out of the question."

Dinner was long over, and he and Iolaus sat by the hearth facing each other. Alcmena was in her corner chair, grinning at them while she sewed a new dress for a village girl who was to be married the following week.

It was a comfortable room. Not so large that voices echoed, or so small that anyone felt cramped. Hangings on the walls and vases filled with flowers lent it color; the hearth provided more than simple physical warmth.

"No," he repeated, just in case Iolaus hadn't heard him the first hundred times.

"But, Herc," his friend protested, "think of the honor. Of the position."

"Of the women?" Hercules suggested.

"Well . . . yes, but that's not the point."

"What, exactly, is the point, then?"

Iolaus looked around the room in frustration before

leaning forward. "The point is, these good and obviously reasonable people think that we, you and I, are responsible and intelligent enough to choose the *one* woman, the *only* woman, the absolute *best* woman among them to serve as their summer queen." He held up the scroll. "It's the highest honor they can bestow upon their citizens. Well, to their women, anyway. And we are the ones who are going to choose her!"

"What's the catch?"

Iolaus made a noise that sounded as if he were being strangled. "Catch? Why does there have to be a catch? We go, we pick, we eat, we drink, we leave. What catch?"

"Right. What's the catch?"

Iolaus slumped back in his chair, nearly defeated. "I don't get it. I just don't get it."

"Neither do I," Hercules said. "That's why I asked you what the catch is."

Iolaus' voice rose as he slapped the scroll against his palm. "There. Is. No. Catch!" He looked to Alcmena quickly. "Sorry. He just makes me crazy sometimes, that's all."

Without looking up from her work, Alcmena gestured an *it's all right, he does that to me, too.*

Hercules pushed a hand through his hair. He was tired of arguing, but he wasn't so tired that he could so easily be swept into another one of Iolaus' schemes. His friend had been trying for what seemed like forever to find a woman for him; not to replace Deianera, but to fill what the man knew was an emotional gap in Hercules' life. Unfortunately, as good-hearted and well meaning as Iolaus was, his eagerness to help sometimes fuddled his brain.

Still, spending a few days by the sea looking at beauty didn't seem all that bad.

This summer festival actually sounded like it might be fun. According to Iolaus, it was an annual celebration, held to ensure that the growing season would produce a rich harvest. Offers to Demeter for her favor on land, and to Poseidon for his on the sea, were accompanied by feasts large and small, parades, street entertainments, and what sounded like a continual round of parties, culminating in the ritual selection of the summer queen.

The problem was the catch.

There was always a catch. A trick. A hidden clause. A corner around which the unexpected lay in wait. Hercules didn't mind surprises in general, just the ones that tended to take off his head.

With Iolaus, such surprises were the rule.

"Listen," he said patiently. "Do you remember the last time you got involved with a beauty contest?"

Iolaus winced.

Hercules laughed. "Artemis, Athena, and Aphrodite, remember? You had to choose between them, and you nearly started a war."

"Wasn't my fault," Iolaus muttered. "Aphrodite tricked me with her damn golden apples." He lifted his head defiantly. "And there are no goddesses involved this time, okay? This will be different."

"Okay," Hercules said cautiously. "Then why us? We've never been there, we don't know anyone there, and we're not related to whoever runs the place."

"Because," Iolaus explained with exaggerated patience, "we are known far and wide for our good deeds, our honesty, and our unimpeachable integrity."

"Of course. I should have known."

Iolaus closed his eyes, breathed deeply several times, and sighed. Loudly. "All right," he said, flopping a hand over in his lap. "I'll go alone. It'll be tough, but I think I can manage it."

Hercules swallowed a laugh. "I think so, too."

For a long moment Iolaus watched the fire. "I hear Themon is a lovely city."

"I'm sure it is," Hercules answered warily.

"Right by the sea."

"Yes, so I've heard."

Iolaus inhaled deeply. "All that fresh air, that salt air." He thumped his chest. "It does something to the appetite."

"Which one?" Hercules asked.

Iolaus gave him a *now that hurt, that really hurt* look, and appealed to Alcmena with a tilt of his head.

"Now wait a minute," Hercules began, sensing a conspiracy in the making.

"I think you should go," his mother said calmly.

"What?"

"See?" Iolaus nodded. "Even your mother thinks it's a good idea."

Hercules scowled. "This isn't fair."

Alcmena kept her face hidden, but he suspected she was grinning. "You need the time away. You need to see Themon; it's as lovely as Iolaus says." She did look up then. "And you need to leave before I have your head for a doorstop."

A glare to Iolaus kept him silent.

"Mother—"

"In the morning," she said, the matter already decided. "You'll be out of my hair, you'll keep Iolaus out of trouble—"

"Hey," Iolaus objected.

"—and then I can really look forward to seeing you again."

There were no doubt dozens of arguments against it, perhaps even a hundred or so, but in the face of Iolaus' eagerness and his mother's calm insistence, he couldn't think of one that sounded like it made any sense. For that matter, at the moment he couldn't think of one at all.

"You two make a good team," he said in reluctant admiration.

"So do you two," she answered. She rose, kissed his cheek, and smiled at Iolaus. "In the morning. I'll have food prepared for you, for the trip."

When she had left, Iolaus did his best not to gloat. "A wonderful woman your mother is. She knows what's good for you, even if you don't." He sat up then, and slapped Hercules' knee. "It'll be all right, you'll see. We'll have a good time, we'll do a little fishing, we'll judge this silly contest, and we'll be out of there before you know it."

"Silly contest? I thought this was supposed to be an honor we can't refuse?"

"Oh, it is," Iolaus agreed, standing, stretching, and yawning. "Really. It is."

He bade Hercules a good night, leaving him to the fire, and the shadows on the wall.

And eventually to a deep sleep.

Yet even in his sleep, Hercules couldn't shake the feeling that someone was watching him.

Not from behind a tree, but from above.

From behind a dark cloud, where storms were born.

"The way I see it," Iolaus said the following afternoon, "we should have no trouble at all deciding who is the most beautiful."

They had made good time after leaving Alcmena's house, taking the generally unused road over low green hills toward the sea. A perfect day with perfect weather, and Hercules was able to take the first few hours of Iolaus' chatter with good humor, and a few knowing gibes.

Now, however, that chatter was beginning to wear a little thin around the edges.

Iolaus had energy enough for a dozen men, two dozen men, and prolonged exposure to it was more exhausting than climbing mountains or fording rivers swollen with winter's melting snow. It had been that way all the years he had known him, and as Iolaus continued with his lecture on the various points of beauty they should consider, Hercules was forced to admit that his enthusiasm was contagious.

It was indeed time to move on.

To spend a few days by the sea, to enjoy a feast or two, to bask in good company and drink good wine ... it would have been churlish of him to refuse. Besides, working on that wall had been getting a little boring.

If Hera was indeed up to something, at least now

he was away from Alcmena, who would be safe.

"Interviews," Iolaus said.

Hercules frowned. "What interviews?"

Iolaus jabbed him with an elbow. "Pay attention, Herc, I'm trying to educate you here. Interviews with the ladies, of course. Don't you think it would be a good idea to have interviews with each of them? To find out if they're worthy of the honor?"

"I—"

"Of course it is. Why, we might even have to take each one to dinner. At the festival's expense, of course. To make sure they understand the gravity of their position. We certainly don't want to dishonor the good people of Themon by choosing a woman who would disgrace them, right?"

"Oh, right. Absolutely." Hercules glanced at the brush-choked hillside on their left, wondering if he might be spared by a rock slide or something.

"It's very important, Herc, that we take our time with this."

"Naturally." To their right, the land sloped down into a meadow. Maybe there was an army down there, hidden in the tall grass, waiting to ambush unsuspecting travelers.

"Of course, if one of them should fall in love with me, that could pose a problem."

Hercules looked up. A lightning bolt, maybe?

"Two would be flattering, though, I suppose."

"Sure."

"Three would be embarrassing. But not unworkable."

"Right."

Iolaus glared at him. "You're not paying the slightest attention to what I'm saying, are you?"

Hercules laughed sheepishly. "I'm sorry, Iolaus." He spread his arms. "I'm just enjoying the view and the trip, that's all."

"That's all right. You just leave everything to me. I'll take care of us."

"Right."

A mile or so later Iolaus stopped. Several paces later Hercules turned around.

"Do you think I'm dressed for the part?"

Iolaus wore, as always, heavy leather vest armor open midway to his stomach, leg coverings, boots, and sword.

"You look fine to me."

"I don't know." He slapped dust from the padded shoulders. "I think maybe they're expecting something more . . . I don't know, elegant." He frowned. "You know what I mean? Robes and such. Like judges wear."

"We're not that kind of judge, Iolaus," Hercules reminded him.

"Still, I don't think we're—*hey!*"

Hercules had grabbed his arm and nearly yanked him off his feet as he propelled him up the road. "We're traveling, Iolaus. We're walking. We get dusty; we get dirty. That's the way of it. When we get to Themon, we'll clean up and we'll look fine."

Hercules' tone left no room for discussion, and he was glad Iolaus didn't pursue the subject. Still, the man muttered for a long time, and kept examining his clothes and shaking his head. At one point, just before they camped for the night, Hercules thought he heard Iolaus say something about a tailor.

There were no dreams that night, no prickling intimations of danger.

Yet Hercules, despite the pleasant weariness after a long day of travel, found it difficult to fall asleep.

It wasn't so much the catch he just knew was involved in this judging invitation as it was a persistent feeling that strings were being pulled. Iolaus claimed he was looking to create problems where there weren't any, and perhaps that was, in some sense, true. But his natural suspicion had saved him on more than one occasion, and he wasn't about to discount it now.

When sleep finally forced his eyes closed, he could have sworn he heard voices floating toward him on the wind.

By the following midday his mood had lifted. Hercules and Iolaus stopped in a village for something to eat, and moved on.

Already the breeze carried a faint hint of salt air, and the hills had begun to level to flatland, leaving wider valleys behind.

Iolaus, however, was curiously silent.

Finally Hercules couldn't take it anymore. "Are you all right?" he demanded.

Iolaus shrugged. "I think so. I didn't sleep all that well last night, I guess."

"Oh? Why?"

He shrugged. "I don't know. Maybe it was because I kept thinking I heard voices."

Hercules stopped.

I knew it, he thought; I knew it.

"What voices?"

Iolaus shrugged again, and didn't stop until he realized Hercules was no longer beside him. When he turned around, it was with eyes narrowed and one hand on the hilt of his sword.

He pointed with his chin. "Those voices, I think."

Hercules didn't have to look. If there were as many men behind him as had stepped onto the road behind Iolaus, there probably wasn't going to be a whole lot of time left for discussion.

5

The bandits were a ragtag lot. Some wore simple clothing; others wore bits and pieces of scarred leather armor. The only things they had in common were their staffs and swords, a dagger or two, and their headgear—a black cloth wrapped around their heads so that only their eyes showed, with the cloth tails tied into a large knot behind their necks.

In the center of each headpiece was a large red rectangle.

Hercules turned to face those behind him, and smiled as genially as he could while he backed up. Slowly.

"Gentlemen," he said, spreading his arms to show he was neither armed nor carrying anything that could even remotely be construed as treasure. "Gentlemen, I don't think this is a very good idea."

The bandit nearest him swept his sword sharply through the air. "Just be quiet," he snarled, "and this'll be over in a minute."

The other bandits growled in agreement.

Unless it was discord. Hercules couldn't tell. The apparent leader was the only one who had bothered to leave a space in his helmet for his mouth.

He stepped back again, and felt Iolaus bump up behind him.

"What do you think?" he asked over his shoulder.

Iolaus drew his sword and ran a judging thumb along its cutting edge. "Well, I suppose, for starters, we could cut off a few heads."

Hercules nodded. "Or we could make them dig their own graves before we hanged them."

Iolaus laughed shortly. "I like that one."

"Hey," the leader snapped. "What are you two talking about?"

"Our plan," Iolaus told him as he eyed the men ranged before him.

"You can't have a plan."

"Why not?" Hercules asked reasonably. "You have a plan, so I think it's only right we should have a plan."

"We don't have a plan."

Iolaus shook his head in disbelief. "He doesn't have a plan."

"I think he does," Hercules said.

"Oh, yeah?" the leader said, snarling and waving his sword again. "If you're so smart, what's our plan?"

Iolaus carved a pattern in the air with his sword. "You're going to ambush us, rob us, and either kill us outright, or leave us here for dead."

The bandits growled something.

The leader hushed them with a wave. "Lucky guess."

Iolaus bowed mockingly.

"But it's a better plan than yours." The man sneered.

"Why?" Hercules said.

"Because there's ten of us and only two of you."

The bandits laughed.

Hercules couldn't help it—he felt sorry for the lot of them. Only the leader looked as if he had any meat on his bones, and their weapons, while no doubt lethal enough, were probably older than most of them. And in not much better shape.

"I'm bored," Iolaus said. He raised his voice. "Now listen, gentlemen, we're on an important mission to Themon. It'll go easier on you if you just let us be on our way."

Hercules nodded his agreement. "We don't want any trouble. Really."

Somewhere in the pack one of the bandits made the sound of a worried chicken.

Hercules felt Iolaus stiffen, and he sighed. He didn't need any special talents to know what that taunt would do.

"Oh, dear," said Iolaus regretfully. "I really do wish you hadn't done that."

Hercules sighed again. Sometimes it was a real pain when he was right.

"Now look," the bandit leader insisted. "You just—"

Iolaus moved first.

With a shriek worthy of a Harpy in a particularly foul mood, he charged the quintet facing him, swinging his sword wildly. They scattered, but not quickly enough for two to avoid being dropped to their knees by the flat of his blade.

At the same time Hercules charged the leader and the other men. The bandit leaped nimbly to one side and urged his men forward. One of them immediately swung a staff that caught the air where Hercules' head would have been if he hadn't ducked, reached up, and snatched the staff away. The bandit blinked, first at the loss of his weapon, then at the smack he received on the temple just before he crumpled to the ground.

A second bandit scurried in front of Hercules and used a two-handed spin of his staff to keep Hercules at bay. The man's arms, however, weren't quite up to the task. One end of the staff hit the dirt, snapped up, and clipped him on the chin.

"Get them!" the leader shrieked in frustration.

Iolaus, meanwhile, found himself with one bandit in front of him, one behind, both with swords that they seemed to know how to use. Their problem was coordination—they charged at the same time, weapons extended like lances, and all Iolaus had to do was wait until the last second, then step aside and use his own sword to deflect theirs into the ground with a single slap. Momentum did the rest—when the blades stuck in the road, the bandits were lifted off their feet and they collided crown to crown.

"Get them!" the leader bellowed in exasperation.

After a check to be sure Iolaus was all right, Hercules sidestepped another charge, grabbed the trailing black cloth tail and spun the man off his feet, released the tail, and sent him tumbling down the slope into the high grass below.

"Get . . ." The leader glanced around, looked at Hercules, and threw up his hands in despair just before he took off down the road. The others soon followed, although not nearly as fast.

When the last of the bandits vanished around the far bend, Iolaus said, "Wow," with a breathless grin. "Now that's a way to break up a day."

"Not very good, were they?" Hercules said, realizing as he examined himself that he hadn't even broken a sweat.

"Oh, no, they were great," Iolaus assured him, posing with hands on his hips. "We were just better, that's all."

Hercules nodded. "Yeah. Sure."

He started up the road, shaking his head. Iolaus was wrong, of course; the bandits hadn't been great at all. To call them mediocre would have been kind. Pathetic, in truth, was more like it. He hoped they didn't intend to make their living as thieves; with skills such as theirs, they would undoubtedly starve before the week was out. Or kill each other off by mistake.

Several hours later they made camp beside a shallow creek. Iolaus hunted their supper and cooked it over a low fire. Stars pricked the night sky. A faint splash disturbed the water.

"I'd like to know something," Iolaus said as they bedded down for the night.

"What?"

"Why do they always come one or two at a time?" Hercules frowned.

"I mean, there were ten of them, Herc. Ten! If they had all come at us at once, we would have had a harder time of it."

It was a point. It seemed that in most battles they found themselves in, the enemy tended to hold back its best advantage.

"Maybe the next time we fight outnumbered, we should point it out to our opponents," Hercules suggested as his eyes closed.

"What, and get ourselves killed? Are you nuts?" Hercules laughed silently.

A minute later Iolaus wondered if maybe they shouldn't sleep in shifts.

Hercules grunted.

"They may come back, you know. They might try to take us under cover of night. It would give them courage, not having to face me. Us."

Hercules grunted.

"I mean, they were pretty awful, when you think about it, but that doesn't mean they won't get lucky if we can't see them to fight them."

Hercules rolled onto his side and draped an arm over his ear.

It didn't work.

"If we're asleep, they could capture us without much trouble. Or kill us."

Hercules grunted, louder.

"Tell you what—maybe I'll just sit up for a while. I'll wake you when I get tired."

Hercules began to count to himself, betting he wouldn't reach fifty.

When he reached twenty he heard the distinct sputter of Iolaus snoring.

"Good night, friend," he whispered. "Sleep well."

Emerald green and thick, a plain of low grass flowed to the horizon without a tree, without a flower.

Nothing moved.

The sky was too blue to look at, without a cloud or bird to mar its surface.

Nothing moved.

Slowly Hercules looked to his right, turning in a complete circle, fingers twitching uneasily at his sides.

Nothing moved.

Without the sun for guidance, he was lost.

He took a step anyway, and his high woven boots made no sound in the grass, and the guards that protected his arms from wrist to elbow reflected no light.

Nothing moved.

No sense of time, no sense of distance. Neither the plain nor the sky changed as he walked, checking from side to side, checking behind him, checking above.

Knowing he was being watched, and growing angry because he could not find the watcher.

And nothing moved until he felt a faint rumbling beneath his soles, a rumbling that threw him off stride and forced him to stop.

The sky darkened.

The grass began to sway.

Ahead of him the ground began to shift, to swell, to rise into a mound from which the grass fell like stones.

The rumbling intensified, a stampede of invisible creatures much larger than cattle.

The mound split open.

The sky darkened further.

A shadow rose slowly from the mound, thick and wide and filling the air with the stench of something that had rotted for centuries at the bottom of the sea.

He took a step back.

The shadow grew.

When the sky turned to storm-ridden night, lightning on the horizon, wind damp with cold rain, he saw the eyes in the shadow.

They were green.

And they watched him.

Though he wanted to run, the eyes held him; though he wanted to cry out, the eyes refused to give him his voice.

When they expanded, he believed at first they were growing. Then he realized the shadow had begun to glide toward him, soundlessly, and there was nothing he could do but stare at the watcher, struggle to move, and widen his own eyes in terror when he saw the white that began to glow below the eyes.

With a groan that sounded almost like a cry he wrenched around and began to stumble through the grass, not looking back, not daring to look back, not even when he felt the stench of the shadow's breath on his back, not even when the ground bucked and rolled, not even when he knew he would not escape.

When at last he fell, he rolled immediately onto his back.

He saw the eyes.

He saw the shadow.

He saw the white glow, and soon saw that it came from the white of the shadow's fangs.

And that's when he heard the quiet, mocking laughter.

"No!" he yelled, and sat up so quickly a cloud of dizziness passed over him. He rubbed his eyes with the heels of his hands, then looked around quickly.

Iolaus was still asleep, snoring. The fire had almost died in its bed. Stars still shone. The moon had begun its slow descent to morning.

There was no monster out there, and no laughter.

He blew out a slow breath and lay down again, cupping his hands beneath his head. Dreams that powerful did not come to him often; when they did, he paid attention.

At the moment he had no idea what the dream meant, or what formed that killing shadow.

But he knew the laughter.

It belonged to Hera.

6

Holix was exhausted.

He was nearly drained of all but the energy to get him to his favorite place above the sea rocks.

Yet it wasn't just the work that tired him; it was the city itself.

The excitement was almost palpable as the festival grew near. Every day, and most of the night, workers cleaned and repaired the walls, replaced worn roof tiles, and swept the streets. Travelers from inland villages and towns had begun to pour into the city, filling every inn and tavern, sleeping in tents on the outskirts, or taking their chances by napping in alleys. Musicians, dancers, and other entertainers practiced in the plaza; flowers were brought in by the cartload to be strung from roof to roof across the boulevard; the slaughterhouses were working overtime; and chefs were practically melting in the heat of their fires.

Even the rebels had kept a low profile.

Holix had never seen anything like it, and when the stable master gave him a break, he made straight for the rocks before all the energy humming through The-mon fried him.

Sadly, he hadn't seen much of his friends lately. But he had heard the great news that both Sana and Cire had been chosen by the council to be among the finalists for the title of summer queen. He was pleased for them, but he was also a little worried.

No one had yet explained to his satisfaction why some of the previous queens hadn't remained in The-mon. Based on what he'd been able to find out, something like every seventh one simply vanished. Asking the stable master had only resulted in him getting his ears boxed, and the gruff man's wife had dismissed his questions by telling him he was still fresh from the country and therefore wasn't capable of under-standing.

As he neared the row of trees, he was surprised to see that someone else was already there. A figure in white, sitting dangerously near the edge of the cliff.

He almost turned around and returned to town; company was exactly what he didn't want right now. It was peace he was after; peace and quiet.

Curiosity pulled him forward, however, and when he reached the trees, he realized the figure was Cire, all hunched over, her face covered by her hands.

Unless it was Sana.

He approached slowly, trying not to startle her but still letting her know she was no longer alone.

She looked up, and he stopped.

Her face shone with tears.

"Holix," she said plaintively, and by the husky voice he knew it was Cire. "Holix, help me."

He hurried over and knelt at her side, and was immediately taken aback when she flung her arms around his neck and began weeping on his shoulder. Awkwardly he slipped an arm around her back and stared out to sea, seeing nothing as he frowned.

Finally he whispered, "What is it?"

She loosened her embrace and leaned away without removing her arms. Her head trembled as she cried, "I don't want to die, Holix. I don't want to die."

Jax made his way quickly through the narrow streets north of the plaza. They were not as crowded as the others; most of the festivities were scattered through the southern, seaward side of the city. Yet there were still enough people here to hide him. His simple clothes marked him as a servant. He was, in effect, invisible, and that suited him just fine.

It was midafternoon when he reached his destination. He was late, but he took several minutes more to make sure he hadn't been followed before slipping into what looked to be an ordinary house.

The woman waited for him.

She was of middle years and, as far as he could tell, youthful appearance, seated as she was in deep shadow on a chair in the far corner of the room. As always, she wore a thin veil over the lower part of her face. He had never seen her in clear daylight, wouldn't know her if he passed her on the street.

He apologized as he entered, and sat on the floor near the entrance, drawing his legs up, hugging his shins.

"No matter," she said. She kept her voice soft.

"Did they do it?" he asked.

She shook her head.

"But there were nearly a dozen of them," he exclaimed angrily. "That has to be enough."

"We're not dealing with ordinary men, Jax. You must remember that."

He scowled. Maybe she was right, but still . . . ten against two ought to have been sufficient odds. Not for the first time he wished he had gone with them. Rotus was a good man, but he had never struck Jax as someone who was capable of leading men into battle.

"So what will we do?"

He could sense her patient smile. "We will try again. There is plenty of time, Jax, plenty of time."

The fingers of his right hand traced a meandering design across the floor by his feet. "What . . ." He took a deep breath. "What if we can't stop them?"

She laughed, but kindly. "Oh, Jax, we won't, don't you know that?"

"What?"

"We won't stop them. We can't."

His scowl deepened. He recognized that he wasn't the brightest young man in the world—Holix, for one, was a whole lot smarter, even if he was a farmer—but he thought he had understood the plan from the outset: prevent Hercules and Iolaus from reaching Themon. As a result, Councillor Titus would have no judges, the summer queen would not be chosen, and the people would rise up in indignation and throw the old fart out of office. Simple.

If Hercules and Iolaus actually got here, and the

51

summer queen was actually chosen, the people wouldn't rise up and throw the old fart out of office. Simple.

So why didn't he get it?

"You'll have to trust me," the woman said. "We've done all right so far, haven't we?"

Well, he thought as he nodded yes, he supposed so. If you count dyeing the council-chamber doors green, and writing really clever incendiary slogans on walls, and passing pamphlets around that suggested Titus hadn't exactly been elected king or anything, and didn't have the best record around, and wasn't it a little suspicious that the man remained in power after nearly twenty years?

The trouble was, the council had liked the new shade of green, the graffiti broke up the monotony of all those boring walls stretching one right after the other, and half the people couldn't read anyway, so the pamphlets were pretty much a wash.

Still, he couldn't find it within himself to complain. After all, she had explained at the start that this revolution business was complicated stuff. Not everything was as it appeared to be.

"I'm confused," he confessed.

"Don't be, dear Jax. Just do what you have to, and I'll take care of the rest."

They spoke for another two hours, planning ways to disrupt the parades and feasts that were to begin the next day. By the time he left, his revolutionary fervor had been renewed, and as he hurried down the street he couldn't stop himself from raising his arms and yelling "Down with the tyrant! Down with Titus!" just for the fun of it.

Hearing his shouts, a nearby cobbler darted out of his shop and looked up at his roof. "By the gods, what happened? Is he stuck?" Not seeing anyone up there, he shrugged, looking baffled.

Jax sighed, shook his head, and hurried on.

Despite what his leader had said, maybe it was about time he got Holix involved.

Holix was bewildered, as well as still exhausted.

Cire had finally stopped crying, but she hadn't stopped clinging to him. Not that he was complaining, he wanted the gods to note, but this wasn't like her at all. Or her sister. Although they were servants for one of the richest families in Themon, they certainly never acted servile around their friends. Their tongues were tart, their humor biting. Despite their own lowly station, they couldn't quite get over the fact that Holix hadn't been born in a city, and they laughed at him for being a country bumpkin.

Until now.

"Cire," he said soothingly, stroking her back and feeling guilty for liking it, "you're not going to die. What makes you think that?"

All too soon she pulled away, plucked a cloth from her long sleeve, and dried her eyes.

"Last night," she said, her voice quavering with emotion, "I heard them talking."

Them; the family she worked for. She seldom called them by name, at least not in his presence. It

53

had nothing to do with the fact that he worked in a stable while she and Sana worked in a fine house; it had everything to do with the fact that she couldn't abide them—husband or wife, or any of their eight children.

"They thought I was asleep."

He waited patiently, thinking he had never seen her so beautiful, here on the hillside, the sunlight caught in her hair, her cheeks flushed and gleaming.

"They were talking about another woman, a queen they had known from many years ago. She . . ." Cire gulped back a sob and lowered her head. "She was found the next morning."

He frowned. This was the first time he had heard that any of the queens had stuck around after the rites and festival. Surely this was a good sign.

Cire shuddered. "Part of her, anyway."

Or maybe not.

His eyes widened. "Part of her?"

She nodded. "Her foot, and some of her leg."

He swallowed heavily. "But that doesn't mean anything, Cire. She must have . . . I mean, she must have . . ." He stared blindly at the water, trying desperately to think of some logical explanation. All he could remember was the fishing boat he had seen, vanishing into the shadow. No one had ever mentioned it, and even he had come to doubt his own eyes.

"Do you remember that boat?" she asked. She had shifted to kneel in front of him, their knees touching. "The one you said you saw the other night? But we didn't see it?"

He nodded.

"*They* were talking about other queens, Holix. You were right—every seven years one disappears. And they . . ." She bit down on her lower lip and shook her head.

He didn't know what to say. Right here was where the summer queen would be enthroned. From this spot, at sunrise, she could see both the sea to the south and, far beyond the trees, the fields to the north. No one would be with her; it was part of the ceremony, part of the blessing of the fruits of the sea and land.

If the rumors were right, this was the seventh year.

"They were all servants, you know," she said.

"All of them? The queens?"

She nodded. "The ones that vanished, yes."

Boldly he reached out and took her hands, tugged at them until she looked up. "That still doesn't mean you're going to die, you know. I mean, maybe you won't be chosen."

She stared.

He blushed. "No, wait, I mean, of course, you'll be chosen. I mean, you're the most beautiful woman I've—" He stopped. He grinned inanely. "I mean, maybe they'll choose Sana. She's—" He stopped. He considered. "I mean, naturally, you're more beautiful than she is, but—"

"We're twins, Holix," she said, smiling shyly.

"Well, yes, of course, you are. But beauty isn't . . . I mean, she's . . . that is to say . . ." He sighed loudly. "I think I'll just go lie under a chariot."

She laughed, leaned over suddenly, and kissed his cheek.

Holix clamped his lips shut. They wanted to kiss her back, they wanted to babble, they wanted to take back the chariot bit, but they only succeeded in emitting a groan.

When she calmed, still holding his hands, she began watching the flight of a gull over the rocks. The tide was on its way in, and waves crashed against them, sending spray and foam into the sunlight.

"There was someone with them," she said, refusing to meet his gaze. "I heard them say they didn't want Sana to win." Her tone turned bitter. "She's too valuable, *they* said. Almost . . . almost like family, *they* said. The other one, the visitor, said a proper donation to the proper gods would probably fix that." She did face him then, her expression hard and dark. "It was Titus, Holix. Titus Perical, and I heard the money change hands."

He almost said, Impossible.

He almost said, You must have been dreaming.

But the look on her face told him he'd be wrong on both counts. Which meant Councillor Titus already knew who would win the summer queen contest. Which meant the judges would only be going through the motions.

"But how?" he asked. "How could he?"

"I don't know," she said in a soft voice. "And I don't care. All I know is, they want me to die. For some reason, I'm going to be the summer queen." She squeezed his hands tightly. "That means a sacrifice, Holix. I'm going to be a sacrifice."

They both looked out at the water, and the afternoon sun turned abruptly cold.

7

The road wound through the low coastal hills. The ground had become more sandy, more rocky, and the brush along the roadside less lush, more prickly. There were few trees to speak of, and an increasing number of gulls filled the air overhead. Themon was not far away, though they didn't, of course, know this. It lay at the southern edge of a plain that began on the other side of a gap that the road vanished into not five miles away.

"I've been thinking," Iolaus said.

"I know."

"You do?"

"Yep."

"How do you know?"

"Because, Iolaus, you've been thinking all day. Aloud. Constantly. I'd have to be deaf not to know you've been thinking."

"Well, if you're so smart, what exactly have I been thinking about?"

Hercules was tired. The sun was warm this close to

the sea, the breeze virtually nonexistent, and the lunch they had had at the last village would have been better if it had been served in the underworld as a punishment for dead gluttons. He hadn't said this, of course, since that would probably have caused some kind of revolution, and he would have been the one to get the blame.

His mood, to be charitable, was a little on the sour side.

"Well?"

He sighed. "All right. First, you thought it would be a good thing if I let you do all the judging. In secret, of course. You figured it would be unfair for someone like me to be part of a contest that involved ceremonies for the gods. A conflict of interest, I believe you called it, right?"

"Right," Iolaus said grudgingly.

"Then you thought that wouldn't work, because then I wouldn't meet any of the ladies in the contest. Which, you claimed, would be bad for me, because I've been alone for too long, and I know that was my mother talking, not you, so we're not even going to discuss it."

"Right," Iolaus said grumpily.

"Then you said—"

"Boy, you really have been listening, haven't you?"

"Hush. I'm doing your thinking, remember?"

"Oh. Right. Sorry."

"Then you wondered about those bandits yesterday. That red design on their masks must mean something, you said, and you've been trying to figure out exactly what that was."

"Well, you never know, Hercules. They might be members of some mysterious army we'd be duty bound to get rid of before they caused too much trouble."

"Them? Trouble?"

Iolaus laughed. "All right. In theory."

Hercules nodded and continued: "Then you decided, if they were really part of some army, we wouldn't have to worry about them because they weren't all that good in the first place. Which, you also decided, meant that the fight we had yesterday must mean something else besides a simple waylaying of travelers."

"Well, that makes sense, doesn't it?"

"I don't know."

"I think it does."

"I know. I heard you. I also heard you wonder why there weren't more people on the road. We're heading in the right direction, and the festival is only a few days away, so we ought to be seeing more people."

"That's right."

"So you wonder if we're late. Or if those bandits have anything to do with it."

"So? That makes sense, too, doesn't it?"

"I guess so. I'm still working out the judging thing."

"Then you'd better hurry up."

"Why?"

"Because they're going to try again."

"What, the judging?"

Iolaus pointed. "No, the fighting."

• • •

Some fifty yards back, the bandits had been hiding in a shallow ditch, camouflaged by branches. As Iolaus pointed they threw their cover aside and boiled onto the road, sprinting toward the two men. Most of them sprinted, anyway. Others limped a little, and one moved at a really fast walk.

Iolaus scowled. "I don't think they're going to split up."

Hercules agreed. Unfortunately it appeared as if the bandits had learned a lesson from their encounter the day before. When Iolaus made to charge, Hercules held out an arm to stop him. "Wait," he said.

At forty yards the bandits, waving their swords and staffs and a couple of clubs, began to yell.

"Not yet," Hercules whispered when he felt Iolaus tense.

At thirty yards the runners had outpaced the limpers and the walker.

Iolaus began to bounce on his toes, slapping his sword from one hand to the other.

"Easy," Hercules cautioned.

At twenty yards the runners slowed down a little to allow the limpers to catch up.

There was doubt in their eyes; Hercules could see it, and when their yelling faltered he could almost hear them wondering why those two fools weren't running away or looking for a boulder or fallen tree for protection.

They were confused.

"Hercules?" Iolaus said, doubt in his voice as well.

The bandits didn't stop.

And Hercules said, "Now!"

He had given himself and Iolaus just enough room to manage a headlong run, but not enough for the bandits to get out of the way.

Hercules snapped his arms out, catching the first two men across the chest and lifting them off their feet. By the time they landed, his head was down and he slammed into the next two with his shoulders, knocking them to the ground as well. Then he whirled and saw Iolaus struggling beneath three of them while two others lay on the road, groaning.

It was almost too easy.

He hurried over and grabbed one bandit by the belt and nape, heaved him off the pile, then grabbed the next by the long tail of his mask. This one he yanked backward, allowing Iolaus to roll to his feet and plant a swift side kick into his opponent's stomach.

"Thanks," Iolaus said, panting.

Hercules gave him an *anytime* wave and turned to face one of the bandits he had already dealt with. The man swayed alarmingly as he tried to decide whether to charge or just throw the sword he carried and hope for the best.

"Don't," Hercules warned.

To his left he heard the sharp ring of blade against blade, glanced over just as Iolaus locked swords with a taller bandit, hooked a foot around the man's ankle, and brought him heavily to the ground. A quick thump with his free hand on the bandit's forehead made sure the man wouldn't move for a while.

Hercules' swordsman still hadn't decided what to do.

"You could leave, you know," Hercules suggested with a *suit yourself* tilt of his head.

The man blinked slowly, looked around at his fallen, moaning companions, and evidently came to the conclusion that he couldn't possibly ache much more than he already did.

He charged—or tried to.

Hercules sighed at his recklessness, and sidestepped when the bandit reached him, slapping his back hard and sending him sprawling off the road.

"Hey!" Iolaus shouted. "Hey!"

Hercules spun, fists at the ready, and saw a trio of bandits racing back down the road. They grabbed two kneeling companions and hauled them along. When he turned back, the others were already stumbling away in the other direction, Iolaus on their heels, yelling, until, at last, he slowed to a halt and let them go.

He sheathed his weapon as Hercules joined him. "I don't get it. I just don't get it."

Hercules took his arm, and they moved to the roadside, where they sat on a grassy rise to catch their breath. "Persistent, though."

"It's dumb, Herc." Iolaus shaded his eyes and peered up the road. "That's twice they've lost."

"And you're not happy?"

"Well . . . no," he admitted reluctantly. "I mean, it's like . . . I mean, they're . . ." He looked up at his friend. "I know this is going to sound silly, but they're no fun. They just don't know how to fight."

"If they did," Hercules pointed out, "we'd probably be dead."

"No, no, I don't think so. Cut a lot, maybe, and

62

bruised a whole lot for sure, but I don't think we'd be dead."

Hercules laughed without a sound. Iolaus wasn't a bloodthirsty man, but he did enjoy a good fight. This band of men, on the other hand, hadn't even made them breathe very hard. It was like swatting a bunch of rambunctious kids.

Iolaus wiped his brow with one arm. "Do you think they'll be back?"

"I don't know." Hercules pushed his hair out of his eyes. "I sure hope not. One of them could get hurt."

"I know," Iolaus said sourly. "Imagine—if I really hurt one of those fools, I'm probably going to feel guilty." He chuckled at the irony, slapped his knees, and stood. Then he grabbed Hercules' arm and hauled him to his feet and back onto the road. "Well, we'd better get a move on. The ladies await, and I don't want to show up with any more bruises than I have to."

"That would be awful."

"Are you kidding? Of course it would. How can I convince them of my sincerity if I look like the survivor of a stampede?"

"You couldn't."

"Absolutely right."

"But how will they know the difference?" Iolaus looked at him, too shocked to speak until Hercules grinned. "A joke, Iolaus, it was a joke."

"Right." Iolaus nodded sharply. "I knew that."

A half mile later he said, "I look that bad, huh?"

Hercules couldn't stop the laughter, which doubled

when he saw the indignant look on his friend's face. He wrapped an arm around his shoulder, shook him a little, and suggested they make their last camp just this side of the gap. A good night's rest, an early start, and they would be in Themon by midday.

"That depends," Iolaus said.

"On what?"

"On whether you keep me up all night with your nightmares. Again."

Hercules said nothing, only gave him a somber look.

"It's Hera, isn't it?" Iolaus gestured wearily to forestall an answer. "You said her name last night."

"You weren't sleeping?"

"No. Not after a while."

For several minutes Hercules kept his own counsel, debating before finally describing his dream, and the feelings he'd had long before Iolaus had arrived at Alcmena's home.

"I knew it," Iolaus said miserably. "I knew it."

"Knew what?"

Iolaus slapped his chest, where he kept the scroll he'd been sent. "I knew this was too good to be true."

"Oh, it probably is. True, I mean."

"Then what does Hera have to do with it?"

Hercules shook his head slowly. "I don't know. Maybe nothing. Maybe I'm just too suspicious."

But he knew Iolaus didn't believe that any more than he did. The dream had been a warning. It didn't matter if it had been sent, or if it was only his own natural defenses on alert.

It was a warning.

Later, after they were bedded down for the night, Iolaus suddenly sat up and exclaimed, "Gods, Herc, you don't think she'll be one of the contestants, do you?"

"What?"

"You know, a disguise or something? A trap?"

Hercules almost considered the possibility, but then laughed it away and reminded Iolaus that exhibiting herself in that way simply wasn't the goddess' style.

Iolaus' relief was almost comical as he lay back, flopping his arms at his sides. "You're right. Thank the stars, you're right."

I sure hope so, Hercules thought, just before the sky exploded.

8

When Hercules next opened his eyes, his first thought had to do with the change in the night sky. The stars looked strange, almost as if they had been replaced by fire. And they kept spinning around.

His second thought had to do with the crushing ache in his skull.

Without thinking, he sat up quickly, and realized his mistake just before the pain blossomed and he passed out.

When he opened his eyes a second time, he didn't move. His vision was blurry, and his head felt as if an ox had taken to walking around inside his cranium.

Ambushed, he thought, chagrined; damn, we were ambushed.

Quietly: "Iolaus?"

A muffled groan was his answer.

Carefully he turned his head to the right and saw Iolaus lying a few feet away. Wherever they were, there was enough light for him to see the caked blood in his friend's hair.

When he tried to move, however, a reedy voice said, "Don't. He's all right. It's not as bad as it looks."

"Speak for yourself," Iolaus muttered.

Relieved, and increasingly angry about letting himself be caught, Hercules levered himself up on his elbows, waited for the world to stop spinning, and took a slow deep breath before sitting up all the way.

As his vision cleared, and finally adjusted to the available light, he saw that he was in a large cave. Well over a dozen torches burned on the dark walls, their smoke curling lazily toward a hole in the ceiling. The center of the floor was cleared, but large rocks and boulders were strewn around the edges, and on them sat the bandits. They wore no armor or masks now, and none, as far as he could tell, held weapons. Not that they needed them. The way he felt and Iolaus sounded, a child could keep them in line with nothing more than a sapling switch.

He sat against a board propped against a low boulder; Iolaus lay nearby on a thick pile of straw and cloth.

Curiously, neither of them was bound.

"Thirsty?"

He looked to his left, to a tall angular figure sitting behind a crude table; on the table was a large dagger.

Hercules nodded gingerly.

One of the bandits slid off his perch and dipped a ladle into a barrel, filled it, and brought it over. Hercules reached for it, but the bandit waggled a finger— *drink, but don't touch.* He complied, and the pounding in his head soon subsided to a dull throbbing.

The bandit nodded and backed away, dipping the ladle again before bringing it to Iolaus.

"We're dead, right?" Iolaus said weakly.

"No," the tall one answered with a hint of a smile.

"I feel like it."

"You'll feel better."

"I hope so, or I'd rather be dead."

During this exchange Hercules studied the cave further without trying to be obvious about it. The entrance was far to his right, a glare of sunlight smearing the edges. There were other tables, large jars, and bundles he assumed were filled with food scattered around the boulders. Ledges protruded from the walls, some holding lanterns, a few holding bandits. The bandits themselves, he realized with a start, were young. All of them. And despite his impressions over the past two days, they did not look particularly ill fed or ragged. Bruised and battered a bit, but not deprived. Against the wall directly opposite him he spotted a neat arrangement of weapons—swords, clubs, and staffs—which did not look anything like the miserable weapons the band had used against him.

This, he thought, is very strange.

A sound above him made him look up over his shoulder. A man sat on a ledge halfway to the ceiling. In his hand he held a bow; in the bow was a nocked arrow.

He waved.

Hercules waved back.

At that moment Iolaus struggled to sit up, moaned, and said, "Who *are* you guys?"

The man at the table said, "We are the TLA."

Iolaus and Hercules exchanged puzzled looks as the bandits stirred.

"The *what*?" Hercules asked.

"The TLA" was the answer. "The Themonian Liberation Army."

Iolaus snorted. "You're . . . rebels?"

A strong murmur of proud assent filled the cave. A few rebels slapped their thighs, a few others held up fists.

"Rebels." Iolaus sighed. "Just my luck."

Hercules pushed both hands back through his hair, pausing only when his fingers touched a lump on his skull. When he checked his hands, he saw no blood. For some reason, this didn't give him much comfort. He pulled up his legs, and froze when he heard the distinct sound of a bolt being placed and locked in a crossbow. He smiled in hopes they'd realize he wasn't about to try anything against such odds, and sat straighter.

Although he attempted several times to engage the man at the table, or anyone else, in conversation, none seemed inclined to talk. Except to each other.

An hour passed.

Another.

When he couldn't take the silence any longer, or Iolaus' snoring after boredom had put him to sleep, he shifted as if to stand. Instantly every rebel turned his attention to him.

Thank you, he thought sourly.

"So," he said to the man at the table, "what are you rebelling against?

"The inhuman conditions and vast cruelties Councillor Titus Perical forces all good Themonians to endure" was the unhesitating response.

"Right, that's right," several rebels said.

"You tell 'em, Rotus!" a squeaky voice urged. "You're doing great! Keep it up!"

Rotus nodded. "Titus has been in power for too long."

"Yeah!" cheered the squeaky voice. "You got it, man, you got it!"

Rotus stood, arms folded across his chest. "He has caused many people many . . . hurts, and . . . and he refuses to allow the people to . . . do things!"

A roar of approval filled the cave.

"You're the best, Rotus, the best!" yelled the squeaky voice.

Hercules looked at Iolaus, who, having woken up, shrugged.

When the cheering died down, Hercules cleared his throat. "So what does that have to do with us?"

"Symbols," Rotus answered immediately.

"Good answer," Squeaky Voice said.

"Symbols of what?"

Rotus glared at him. "Symbols of the high-handed way Titus runs the city without the permission and proper designation of the people he's supposed to serve!"

As the cheering swelled again, Hercules, with one eye on the rebels to be sure he wouldn't be skewered, scooted closer to Iolaus. "Are you all right?" he said, wincing at the dried blood.

"I've had worse headaches." Iolaus made a pained

face to prove his point. "But these guys are nuts."

"I heard that!" yelled Squeaky Voice. "He insulted you, Rotus. He impugned your honor!"

"Who *is* that guy?" Iolaus inquired, frowning.

"I don't know," Hercules said. "A Rotus rooter, I guess. But I sure wish he'd shut up."

"I heard that, too!" Squeaky Voice squeaked. "I heard that!"

The cave quieted.

Rotus picked up the dagger and tapped its point on the table. "You're supposed to take part in the summer festival. If you do, nothing will change, and Titus will go on as always. So . . ." He spread his arms and grinned. "You stay here until it's over."

"What?" Iolaus tried to jump to his feet, staggered halfway there, and fell back on his rump. "You can't do that!"

Rotus shrugged. "We already have. You're here, you're not going anywhere, and the festival begins in the morning."

"Well put, well done!" Squeaky Voice cried.

Iolaus rolled his eyes. "By the gods, will you please be quiet?"

Suddenly someone raced across the floor and skidded to a halt in front of him, hands on hips, fiercely scowling, and wearing a black patch over one eye. "*You* be quiet," the rebel squeaked. "You're the prisoner, big boy, not me."

Hercules looked away before he laughed.

Iolaus could only gape and stammer.

The rebel was a woman. Most definitely a woman.

Blond hair a-tangle over her brow, large blue eyes—one of them, anyway—and a dirt-smudged pug nose lightly sprayed with freckles.

Somewhat flustered, Iolaus brushed a lock of hair from his eyes and offered an apologetic smile.

To Hercules' astonishment, she blushed and stomped away to the table, taking the chair Rotus had used, spinning it around, and sitting on it, her arms draped over the low back.

"You'll have to forgive Venitia," Rotus said flatly. "She tends to lose her temper a lot."

Hercules noticed that there were at least two other women in the group, a fact that had evidently not escaped Iolaus' eye either.

"No problem," Hercules said reasonably. "But I don't think holding us here is going to do you any good."

"Really? And why not?"

"We're only judges," he explained. "If we don't show up, they'll only pick someone else in our place."

"They wouldn't dare," Venitia declared, thumping the table with a fist.

"Why not?"

"Because," she answered sharply.

The other rebels grumbled loudly.

"Look," Hercules said, concentrating on Rotus, "we don't have anything to do with this Councillor Titus. Or with Themon, for that matter. My friend Iolaus, here, accepted an invitation, and we intend to honor it."

The grumbling grew louder.

Patience, he told himself; patience.

He tried again: "Since you obviously know who we are, you must also know our reputations." He frowned, and the grumbling subsided. "So why not let us go to Themon, do what we promised, and if we find that your complaints are just, maybe then we can lend you a hand."

"Hey, we're doing all right on our own," Venitia snapped.

The grumbling grew still louder.

"Well, of course you are. I didn't say you weren't."

The grumbling subsided.

Rotus shook his head. "That all sounds pretty good, but we have our orders, and we know what to do." He almost seemed sincere when he added "Sorry."

Iolaus, who apparently couldn't take his gaze off Venitia, nudged Hercules with an elbow. "What's the big deal about a councillor? He's not a king, is he?"

"No," Rotus answered as he perched on the edge of the table. "He's a tyrant."

"You can say that again," Venitia muttered.

Now Hercules was truly puzzled.

Although lands were ruled by kings or other nobles, a number of cities were governed, as was Themon, by councils chosen from the ranks of the rich and educated. Which, these days, pretty much amounted to the same thing.

In times of war, however, when it was clear a strong hand was needed to raise and train an army, the council elected a tyrant to run things. He was a man with sweeping powers whose sole mandate was to protect the city, win the war, and save the people. When the war was over, the parades done, and the booty divided, the tyrant stepped down and the council returned to power.

Almost always.

Rotus nodded at the expression on Hercules' face. "That's right. Themon had a war with pirates a long time ago. Titus was elected tyrant, defeated the pirates . . . and stayed in power."

"How long?" Hercules asked.

Rotus closed one eye and stared at the ceiling, sniffed, held up one hand, stared at his fingers, closed the other eye, bowed his head, opened his eyes, and said, "Twenty years, give or take."

"What?" Iolaus scratched his cheek. "Twenty years? Why hasn't he been replaced?"

The grumbling modulated to a discontented mumbling.

Rotus mumbled something himself, and Hercules asked him, politely, to speak up.

"Because things have been pretty good, that's why," the rebel snarled grudgingly. "Nobody wants to take a chance on changing the government, because they don't want to rock the boat."

"Not *that* good," Venitia corrected.

"Well, yes, not that good," Rotus agreed.

"Right!" someone called. "Not all that good. Pretty awful sometimes, actually."

The others agreed. Loudly. With lots of fist waving and lots of foot stomping. Within seconds, someone had begun to sing what was clearly a song meant to

74

inspire revolutionary fervor. Seconds later all the rebels joined in and were singing. Loudly. With lots of fists waving and lots of feet stomping.

Hercules and Iolaus looked at each other.

"You're sure I'm not dead?" Iolaus asked.

Hercules shook his head, although he himself had decided he was probably still asleep, that this was yet another one of those portentous dreams whose meaning he was expected to decipher so that he could, upon awakening, figure out what to do next. The problem was, all this yelling and grumbling and top-of-the-lung singing was giving him a splitting headache on top of the one he already had.

When Iolaus nudged him sharply with an elbow, he sighed. He was awake. Very awake.

Iolaus leaned close. "Herc, we have to get out of here."

"I know."

"We can't disappoint those ladies."

"I know."

"I mean, they're depending on me, Herc. *Us*. To give them the elusive dream they've always dreamed of since they were children—being the summer queen. Being the queen of Themon. Being—"

Hercules snapped a finger against the man's chin to shut him up. "That was in the invitation, wasn't it?"

Iolaus scowled, rubbed his chin, opened his mouth to protest Hercules' doubt of his command of the language, not to mention his sincerity, changed his mind, and nodded.

The singing continued.

An excruciating hour passed as song followed song, during which Hercules figured this *had* to be Hera's revenge.

Eventually Iolaus nudged him again. "I have a plan."

Of course, Hercules thought; you always have a plan.

"So tell me something I don't already know," he said.

"They have horses."

Hercules stared at him in disbelief. "They what?"

"Horses. That's why they keep leaving. To take care of the horses." Iolaus inched closer. "So we get out of here, grab a couple of horses, and ride." He smiled.

Hercules smiled back. "How do we get out of here?"

Iolaus' smile broadened. "That's your job. I thought of the horses." When Hercules made to snap his chin again, he laughed. "No, really, I have a plan for that, too." He glanced around at the singing rebels. "When I tell you, run for the exit."

"All right," Hercules said doubtfully. "When do we do this?"

"Now!" Iolaus shouted, leaped to his feet, and raced away.

Stunned, Hercules sat for a second, then groaned, leaped to his own feet, and followed Iolaus toward the exit.

Stunned, the rebels kept singing until they realized that their hostages had escaped, then changed the singing to a lot of shouting and screaming and grabbed their weapons before racing for the exit.

It was the bowman on the ledge who scored the first hit.

9

As Hercules and Iolaus exploded from the cave an arrow ricocheted off one of the Hephaestus-forged black guards Hercules wore on each arm from wrist to elbow. The hit startled him, nearly made him stumble, and reminded him that these bandits were not the bumblers he had once believed.

The cave was at the base of a low grassy hill. Ranged in front were a number of stunted trees, and beneath one were a half-dozen horses. Iolaus made straight for them, leaping over an arrow that thudded into the ground just ahead of him. Another hummed past Hercules' left ear, but he didn't turn; that would only delay him, and make him an easier target.

Moments later Iolaus leaped nimbly onto the back of a roan, grabbed her mane, and was gone. Hercules, who wasn't all that fond of horses except when they were pulling things he was riding in, found a larger animal, a black, and threw himself onto its back. Then he scattered the other animals before racing off after his friend.

The last he saw of the rebels, they had reached the trees, some trying futilely to catch the remaining horses, the others impotently shouting their anger while shaking their fists and weapons. It was clear there was no way they'd be able to catch him before he reached Themon.

He should have been relieved.

What he was, was puzzled.

By then, Iolaus had slowed his mount to a canter. His face was red with laughter and excitement, and when Hercules joined him, he reached out to slap his arm.

"Amazing!" he said with a self-congratulatory grin. "Wasn't that amazing?"

Hercules scowled. "I thought you had a plan."

"That *was* the plan."

" 'Run!' was the plan?"

"Sure."

Hercules couldn't believe it. "What kind of a plan is that? Run? That's a plan?"

"What are you complaining about? It worked, didn't it? We're free, aren't we?"

Refusing to give him the satisfaction of a reply, Hercules held out his left arm and pointed to a small scratch at the top of the arm guard. "An arrow, Iolaus. One more inch and I would have been hit."

A nod conceded the point. "But it didn't, Herc. It didn't."

"Yes, but—"

Iolaus laughed, whooped, and urged the roan on to a faster gallop, waving over his shoulder. "Come on,

Herc, we only have a couple of hours before sunset, and the ladies await!''

All right, Hercules admitted, so it didn't get me. So we got away. So it worked. But . . . run? He calls that a plan?

Yet he couldn't help a brief smile of his own, at his friend's exuberance, and at the day itself.

Under a flawless blue sky the plain rolled gently southward, the expanse of short rich grass broken only by the farms and pastures that could be seen in the distance, east and west. Wildflowers added spots of vivid color. Here and there, a full-crowned tree or two loomed over streams or ponds, providing shade and shelter to grazing cattle. With the hills now behind them, the salt air was sharp, energizing, and Hercules spotted a number of gulls wheeling slowly overhead; and higher still, a pair of hawks.

He inhaled deeply, and his headache finally vanished. Maybe, he thought with mental fingers firmly crossed, this journey wasn't going to be so bad after all.

Iolaus waved to him from the top of a rise. He waved back and rode on, ignoring the thumps the horse's spine gave to his rump.

''There!'' Iolaus declared when Hercules joined him. ''Themon, Herc! Our destiny awaits!''

Below them was a wide, well-traveled road. Although not crowded, there were plenty of riders, walkers, and carts and wagons, all streaming toward the city in the middle distance. It wasn't the largest city Hercules had ever visited, but it was refreshing to see such a place unmarred by confining walls, or army camps on the outskirts. Red-tile roofs caught the sun brightly; building walls of varying soft colors glowed; and where the sky curved down to the horizon, he could just make out the glint of the sea.

He looked at Iolaus and smiled warmly. "I have to admit—this was a good idea."

Iolaus preened. "Of course it was. Did you ever doubt me—and don't spoil it by answering."

Hercules didn't, with a laugh.

According to the invitation, the next step, Iolaus explained as they joined the others on the road, was to go straight to a place called the plaza. There they would find the council chambers, meet with Councillor Titus, receive their instructions, and bask in the adulation of the townfolk.

Hercules looked at him askance. " 'Bask in the adulation'? Is that in the scroll, too?"

"No. I made that up myself. Not bad, huh?"

"Don't tell me—you're practicing to be a judge."

Iolaus nodded emphatically. "Absolutely. I don't want them to think I'm some kind of lout, you know."

Hercules wiped a hand over his face. "In case they want to invite you back?"

Iolaus lifted a shoulder. "I don't know. Maybe. Frankly, it never occurred to me."

Right, Hercules thought.

Abruptly the plain gave way to the city, and they found themselves riding down stone-paved streets somewhat wider than those they were used to. Decorations were everywhere, and merchants hawked their wares from stands in front of their shops; the air was thick with the aromas of cooking food, and despite the noise of pedestrians and sellers, music could be heard escaping from the open doors of taverns and inns. The din and the sheer numbers of people made the horses nervous, and it was all Hercules and Iolaus could do to keep them from bolting.

Their pace grew slower as they neared the city's center, where, since Themon had evidently been laid out in a grid, the intersections were particularly crowded.

Not so crowded, however, that Hercules wasn't able to spot the occasional pair of soldiers stationed at the corners. At first he figured they were there to look for rebels; then, after witnessing a brief struggle with a trio of men who had obviously been testing each other's wine-tasting capacities, he realized the soldiers were there primarily to keep the peace.

Evidently Themon was determined that its citizens and visitors would enjoy a festival unmarred by violence.

Suddenly a child darted in front of Iolaus, who had to fight to keep his horse from rearing. It was one thing to escape from their captors without saddle or reins, quite another to keep the animals under control without such aids under conditions like this.

"That's it," Hercules said, sliding to the ground. "We're getting rid of these beasts before they kill someone. Like me."

With one hand still gripping the black's thick mane, he spotted a stable down a narrow, nearly empty side street and made straight for it, not bothering to check to see if Iolaus was following. As he approached, a young man stepped out of the dark interior, wiping his hands on a towel tucked into his belt.

"There's no room," he said regretfully. "We're all boarded up."

"I don't want to board him," Hercules said. "You can have him."

The stable boy blinked his bewilderment. "You . . . I . . ."

"Can have him," Hercules repeated. And as Iolaus rode up he added, "That one, too." Without waiting for permission, he guided the black inside, grabbed a rope from a hook on the wall, and looped it loosely around the animal's neck. "He's been ridden hard, by the way, so take care of him, all right?"

The young man was too flustered to object when Iolaus did the same with his mount.

Hercules smiled and shook his hand. "Thanks. And tell your boss he can do whatever he likes with them, except treat them badly." He leaned forward and deepened his voice. "I'll know if he does."

The young man stepped back with a nervous nod, nearly yelped when Iolaus poked him in the back.

"We have to get to the plaza. Can you tell us how?"

The stable boy nodded again, rattled off directions that made Iolaus blink in confusion, then stopped, excused himself, and repeated the directions more slowly.

"You got that, Herc?" Iolaus asked when the stable boy had finished.

Hercules nodded. He was fairly sure he had understood, but the smell of the stable was a little over-powering, and what he wanted was fresh air. Even the fresh air of the city street. If he made a mistake and got lost, they could always ask someone else. He thanked the stable boy and hurried outside. They were the only pedestrians.

"Left," Iolaus said when he joined him.

"Right," Hercules said.

"No. Left."

"Right."

Iolaus grinned. "See?" And took a step to the left before Hercules grabbed him.

"I said right, not left."

"But I said left, and you said right."

"That's right."

Iolaus made a noise deep in his throat. "I said—"

Hercules stopped him by taking hold of his vest and pulling him close. "Don't start, Iolaus, or we'll be at it all night."

"But what did I say?"

"Too much. Just follow me."

Iolaus started to argue, stopped, and looked over his shoulder.

Hercules did the same.

The stable boy stood in the wide doorway, staring.

"Yes?" Iolaus said warily.

The young man pointed. "Are you . . . Hercules?" he asked hesitantly.

"Nope. I'm Iolaus. Judge Iolaus, that is." He slapped Hercules' arm lightly. "This is Hercules."

The boy gaped. "*The* Hercules?"

Hercules didn't know how to respond to the boy's

tone of awe, so he simply nodded. After all this time on the road, he knew he should be used to people's reactions when they met him, but it still made him uncomfortable. Very often stories of his exploits were, to say the least, considerably embellished by the time he caught up with them, and nothing he could say could convince people otherwise. They believed what they wanted to.

"Wow," the young man said.

Iolaus chuckled under his breath and gave Hercules a nudge. "What did I tell you?" he whispered. "Famous."

The stable boy frowned as he scratched through his thick brown hair. "So you're going to decide who's the summer queen?"

"Right again," Iolaus said proudly. "Now look, we'd love to stay and chat, but we—"

"You're going to kill her," the young man accused quietly. Then loudly: "You're going to kill her!"

Hercules and Iolaus exchanged confused looks, but their questions went unasked when the young man vanished into the stable's dark interior.

Iolaus scratched his head. "City people are weird," he concluded.

He might have said more, but an angry shout interrupted him.

It was the stable boy, charging them with a pitchfork in his hands.

Iolaus barely managed to sidestep the tines, and Hercules didn't have time to think—he stepped to his left as he grabbed the shaft and pulled it to yank the young man off his feet. The stable boy's momentum carried him headfirst into the wall across the street.

The wall didn't give.

"Ouch," Iolaus said with a sympathetic wince.

Stunned, the stable boy looked at him, blinked once very slowly, and began a slow collapse.

In two quick strides, Hercules was beside him. He scooped him up in his arms and carried him into the stable, where he placed him on a bed of straw.

"What was that all about?" Iolaus asked.

"I don't know. Get some water."

Iolaus searched until he found a bucket and a ladle. When he gazed down at the unconscious boy, he looked at the ladle and simply tossed it over his shoulder before emptying the bucket on the boy's head.

The boy sat up instantly, sputtering and yelling.

Hercules put him down again with a firm hand against his chest, waiting patiently until the young man grumbled into a sullen silence.

"Explain," Hercules demanded gently.

The stable boy glared.

Iolaus stood at the young man's feet, one hand grasping his still-sheathed sword. "You heard him. What's going on?"

A long moment passed before the young man said, "My name is Holix, and you're going to kill the woman I love."

10

Shadows began to drift into the streets.

Lanterns on posts and overhanging roofs kept the major streets alight while side streets and alleys slipped into dusk.

Hercules and Iolaus strode purposefully toward the center of the city, not speaking, ignoring the pedestrians who drifted from shop to shop, inn to inn. Their numbers were fewer now, mostly latecomers searching for a place to sleep. In preparation for the next day's festival, the city had grown quiet, as if gathering its energy for the celebrations to come.

The plaza was nearly deserted.

A few workmen still scrambled over the stands that had been constructed on the open square's east and west ends, making sure the seats wouldn't collapse under the weight of those who'd be privileged enough to use them. Strands of blossoms, from orchids to daisies, had been festooned between the pillars. The tiles and paving stones were being scrubbed one last time. More torches, more lanterns were lit, their glow brightening as the sun neared the horizon.

The two men paused as they left the boulevard.

On the far side they saw a group of ten men at the top of eight wide steps, standing beneath an elaborately carved roof.

"The council," Iolaus guessed. There was little enthusiasm left in his voice.

Hercules said nothing.

By the time Holix had finished his story—and had asked, somewhat meekly, if he could sit up, his back was killing him—Hercules had already run through most of his darker emotions. It had taken only a handful of pointed questions to convince him that the young man wasn't lying. He had no doubt then that his suspicions had been well founded, that this year Themon's festival had been turned into one of his stepmother's devious traps.

But he needed more information, and there was only one person who could tell him what he had to know. First, however, there was the council to face.

"You know," Iolaus said, "we could always leave. I think it'd be a lot easier facing those rebels again."

Hercules shook his head. "We can't. We're here now."

"I know we're here now, but we don't have to be here later."

"Yes, we do."

Iolaus sighed. "Yeah, I guess you're right." As they walked toward the men he brightened. "We'll still get to see the contestants, though, right?"

Hercules nodded, with a brief smile.

"That's okay, then."

As they approached the steps one of the men, wearing a voluminous dark-green robe edged with gold thread, turned toward them and scowled. He was of medium height, with thick white hair except for a few strands of black over the ears. His face was lined, but pleasantly so. It was the eyes that struck Hercules— very dark, and set deep beneath dark eyebrows.

"What do you want?" the man demanded. "No one is supposed to be here until the morning."

A soft clank of metal made Hercules aware of the guards posted behind each pillar. Unlike the rebels, these men were well armed and well armored.

"I'm Iolaus," Iolaus announced stoutly, posing with one foot on the bottom step, one hand on his hip. "Your festival judge. You sent for me, remember? And this is Hercules, your other judge."

The council members stirred, whispered among themselves, and did everything but point and ask for an autograph.

Titus Perical hushed them with a sharp gesture, and his welcoming smile reminded Hercules of an aged wolf that hadn't eaten in a very long time.

A languid, beckoning hand invited the two men up the steps, and after the introductions were made and the fussing had died down, Titus put a friendly hand on Iolaus' shoulder.

"You're late, my friend," he said. "We were all concerned for your safety."

"A little scrape with some rebels, that's all," Iolaus said.

The councillors murmured alarm; Titus hushed them again, with a look.

"You're not hurt, I trust?"

Iolaus laughed. "No, not us. I'm not so sure about the rebels, though."

The councillors laughed their appreciation of his courage, and Titus explained apologetically that the rebels—this particular band anyway—were more of a nuisance than a true danger. They certainly wouldn't be allowed to disrupt the ceremonies. And the identity of their leader was close to discovery.

"This band?" Hercules said.

"Yes. They do show up once in a while. Misguided youth who want to rule the world."

And you don't, Hercules thought; could have fooled me.

"We have a pretty fair idea who they are," the man continued. "They'll be under control in no time." He gestured dismissively. "Pests. As I said."

The conversation turned to accommodations for the city's honored guests, and a brief explanation of their expected duties and appearances. As it turned out, in return for covering all their expenses, and a generous pouch of dinars for their trouble, all they had to do was make themselves available to the people for admiration, sit with the council at the banquet just before sunset the next day, and be present for the judging that evening.

"And the ladies?" Iolaus asked innocently.

Titus waggled a mock-scolding finger. "Now, Iolaus, we wouldn't want them to try to bribe you, would we?"

Iolaus looked shocked. "Well, no, of course not."

"Then the minute you see them will be the minute they see you first. At the contest." A pious look skyward. "We wouldn't want to offend the gods by giving unfair advantage, now, would we?"

Iolaus didn't respond until Hercules jabbed the small of his back. "No! Gods, no, that wouldn't be right."

"Of course." Titus glanced at the council. "Now, sirs, if you will excuse us, we have much to do before tomorrow."

Iolaus agreed, made sure he knew the directions to the inn where he and Hercules would be quartered, and shook hands all around. Hercules followed suit, and trailed Iolaus down the stairs.

"Oh. Hercules," Titus called.

Hercules turned.

"Do be careful, won't you? Once those rebels discover you're actually in town, they may try something . . . harmful. I certainly wouldn't want anything to happen to you. Or your friend, of course."

"I think I can take care of myself, but thanks for the warning," Hercules answered, then waved a farewell, and caught up with Iolaus midway across the plaza.

"You know, Herc," his friend said with a sad shake of his head, "this isn't going to be as much fun as I thought. And that guy gives me the creeps."

Hercules couldn't resist a little good-natured teasing. "But what about all those women? Their dreams. Their aspirations. Their hopes. Their—"

"All right, all right," Iolaus groused. "Boy, a guy can't say anything around you, can he?"

Hercules draped an arm around his shoulders as they left the plaza for the boulevard. "Iolaus, you're forgetting something."

"What."

"This city is probably filled with lovely women. This city is about to explode with parties and banquets and parades and who knows what else? This city knows who the fantastic Iolaus is and will—"

Iolaus stopped him with an upraised hand. "Got it, got it, I got it. I'm being greedy, right?"

"Right."

"I should make my own fun, right?"

"Right."

"I shouldn't have any trouble lining up a couple of real—"

The hand that was on his shoulder shifted to cover his mouth. "Don't push it, Iolaus. Don't push it."

Five minutes later they reached the Red Boar Inn, a fine-looking establishment with, Iolaus noted instantly, amazing proximity to other fine-looking inns from which sounds of revelry drifted into the night air. As he made for the entrance, however, Hercules stopped him.

"Take care of the rooms," Hercules told him. "I'll see you later."

Iolaus frowned. "Hey, you're not going to have fun without me, are you?"

"No. I promise." His expression darkened. "But there's someone I have to see, and I have to see him now."

Iolaus shrugged. "I'll go with you."

"No, I don't think so."

Iolaus shifted, ready to argue, until suddenly he realized what Hercules meant. "Oh. Okay. I'll take care of everything, don't worry." His hand touched Hercules' arm. "Just promise me that you're not going to try to take on Hera on your own."

Hercules could so promise, and did. "But it's not Hera I'm looking for," he added. A hearty slap on Iolaus' shoulders sent him back. "Just make sure there aren't any rebels in my bed when I get back."

Then he walked down the boulevard.

Heading for the sea.

Titus paid no attention to the others as they bid him a good night. He kept his gaze on the two men leaving the plaza, wondering if perhaps he had made a mistake. Although there was nothing spectacular about Hercules' appearance, he couldn't help feeling the sheer *power* that emanated from the man.

Even if he didn't know of his connections to the gods, he'd have to be an idiot not to at least sense something beyond the ordinary run of mortals in him.

Hercules was human, and something more.

Just looking at him made Titus uneasy.

Soft footsteps behind him made him smile, and he held out his hand without looking. A much softer hand took his and squeezed it gently.

"Your people," he said, "couldn't hold them, it seems."

A woman's quiet laughter made him smile himself. "They weren't supposed to, darling."

"Did you tell them that?"

"Of course not. But twice, three times their number

wouldn't have done it. I just wish the delay had been longer. I think—'' She exhaled loudly. ''I think he might have too much time to think.''

Titus considered the notion, and dismissed it. ''No. He's not the most friendly man I've ever met—that runt did most of the talking—but I'm beginning to think Hercules is overrated.''

The woman squeezed his hand again before slipping an arm around his waist. ''He didn't make you nervous?''

''Me?'' He laughed silently. ''Don't be silly.''

''You're sweating, my love.''

''It's a warm night.''

''You're tapping your foot.''

Titus looked down, saw his left foot tapping the ground, and ordered it to stop. It ignored him. He shifted his weight as casually as he could. The foot tapped a few more times, and gave up just as he began snapping the fingers of his right hand.

The woman giggled, and leaned her head against his arm. ''You're really not cut out for this sort of thing, are you?''

''What are you talking about?'' he demanded, trying to sound insulted and commanding. ''I've been doing it for years.''

''No, my love,'' she said tenderly. ''You've been making all the speeches. I've been doing all the rest.''

He turned within the circle of his wife's arm, put his arms around her, and said, ''You think this is really the end, that she'll really let us go and''—he gazed out at the plaza—''spare the city?''

Jocasta Perical looked up into her husband's eyes.

94

"I think we should get out before Hera fries us."

He glanced apprehensively at the sky. "You think she would? After all those promises?"

"In a Spartan minute."

He pondered, he thought, he debated, and he snarled when the tapping returned to his foot. "Maybe we should pack, then."

Jocasta smiled. "Darling, what do you think I've been doing all day?"

The city was behind him, nothing but stars overhead and the silver trail of the moon rippling on the water.

The tide was out, and Hercules had no problem making his way between the huge boulders that marked the west end of the beach. Once past them, he walked on for almost another hour, not stopping until he was positive he would not be seen or heard, inadvertently or otherwise.

He also made sure that the way inland wasn't impeded by rocks or cliffs, marshes or thick woodland. Just a precaution, in case he had to run like hell if the meeting went sour.

Stalling, a voice mocked in singsong; you're *stalling*.

So what? he answered grumpily. If I stall long enough, maybe I can talk myself out of it.

He had no idea, not really, why he had come up with this plan in the first place. It was foolish, it was potentially dangerous, and it was probably a waste of time. If he had confided in Iolaus, his friend would have suggested that he was, without question, out of his little demigod mind.

Still, if Holix was right, and if his own impression of Titus Perical was right as well, he and Iolaus would need as many advantages as they could get. Without them, there was a good chance Hera would win this time.

Stalling.

He groaned in unabashed self-pity, stopped, and finally faced the water. Took a deep breath and moved forward until he was in up to his knees, the low waves nudging him, the moon bathing him in cold light.

He spoke a word then, one not in any language any mortal could understand.

Actually, he whispered it.

It didn't make any difference.

Less than a minute later he muttered, "Oh, boy," at the way the sea began to churn.

11

Hercules took an uncertain step backward.

Where the sea had begun to churn, a dome of water pressed upward, slowly, silently, as though a mountain were about to rise from the bottom. Sparks flared from the sides as the tower of water grew. Sparks within the tower raced in dizzying spirals from bottom to top.

Low waves rushed from the tower's base and slammed against his legs, forcing him back until he turned and struggled to the beach's wet apron.

When he looked, the tower was three times his height and still growing. Waterfalls thundered down each side from a central point at the top, looking in the moonlight like rivers of flowing ice.

There was a shadow inside, a deepening black that filled the whole tower.

Hercules waited; there wasn't much else he could do.

Except maybe run, but it was probably too late for that.

When at last the sea tower reached fifty feet into the air and the sea churned and boiled at its base, the water began to slide away from the shadow. Slowly. Bubbles of foam floating away like tiny stars, the waves reversing themselves to shatter against the base.

All of it without a sound.

The water continued to fall, as if sculpting the shadow—head and broad shoulders first, then sculpted chest and muscled arms, finally the waist and legs. On the featureless head was a crown, in the left hand a trident, in the right something else Hercules couldn't make out.

The sea calmed.

The figure looked down.

"Oh," it said in mild, pleasant surprise. "It's you."

Hercules nodded, and waved an apprehensive greeting.

Instantly the figure began to shrink so rapidly that Hercules had to turn away to keep from getting nauseated. When he looked back, the figure was only a head or two taller than he, using the trident's base to push itself toward the beach.

"Hello, Uncle," Hercules said, still unsure if he was welcome or not.

"It's been a while," Poseidon replied. In the moonlight it was difficult to tell his age. His voice was an old man's, but his physique denoted tremendous power. "Sorry about the display there. I thought you were some high priest trying to score points with a divinity. Scares the hell out of them, usually." He held out his right hand. "Tuna sandwich. You want some?"

Hercules chuckled. "No, thanks, Uncle. You eat tuna?"

Poseidon shrugged. "I rule them, doesn't mean I don't get to eat them now and then. They're dull, anyway. Like clams. It's a rule of the sea, Hercules— you absolutely cannot have a good conversation with a clam."

Hercules waited.

"Oysters, now, they're different. Every once in a while they come up with a real pearl of wisdom."

Hercules groaned.

Poseidon laughed, and began to walk east, gesturing his nephew to get moving or be left behind.

Hercules got moving. Poseidon was well aware of his nephew's anger at Zeus, and had judiciously refrained from taking sides. Sympathy was there, however; Hercules sensed it each time they met. In the manner, in the careful choice of words . . . in the way Poseidon hadn't flattened him into the sand or punctured him with the trident for interrupting his dinner.

"Lovely evening," the sea god said, admiring the sky flowing with bright stars. "I really should get up here more often. Starfish don't quite have the same panache, if you know what I mean."

Hercules said nothing. His uncle moved with the languid motion of the sea. Nothing would hurry him. Sooner or later he'd want to know why he was called. Patience was required.

"Alcmena is well?"

"Very well, thanks, Uncle."

"And your friend? Iolaus?"

"As always."

Poseidon finished his tuna in a gulp, spat onto the beach some bones that immediately formed an unidentifiable creature, and said, "Let 'em figure that one out, harebrained mortals."

He meant the scholars who insisted on trying to learn what made the sea do what it did, without taking Poseidon's sometimes whimsical nature into consideration. It was the god's delight to throw them a curve once in a while, just to confuse them.

The night was cool, the sea breeze gentle. In the distance the sky glowed faintly with Themon's light.

"I give up," Poseidon finally said.

"Hera," Hercules told him.

Poseidon stopped, looked down at him, and shook his head. "Considering my position, Nephew, I really shouldn't get involved." A ghost of a smile flitted across his lips. "What'd you do to piss her off this time?"

"Nothing."

"Of course not. Except for a couple of Nereids of my acquaintance, that woman holds a grudge longer than anyone I've ever known. Including humans, I might add." With a nod they began walking again. "So what does this have to do with me?"

"Themon's summer festival."

Poseidon stopped again. "You're involved with that?"

Hercules cocked his head in a shrug. "The council invited Iolaus to be a judge, and wanted me to come with him. As a judge, too."

Poseidon sighed knowingly. "And you came to keep him out of trouble."

"Well . . . mostly, yes."

The sea god laughed, a deep-throated rumbling less heard than felt. "They teamed up against you, didn't they, your mother and your friend? Meet women. Get a home life. Right?"

Grudgingly Hercules nodded. "Something like that."

"Women." Said with both mild condemnation and much affection. "Amazing what they'll do."

Amazing isn't the word for it, Hercules thought; scary is more like it.

Poseidon stabbed the air with the trident. "So? What?"

Hercules hesitated. This was the tricky part: explain without insulting.

"I can't read minds," his uncle said good-naturedly. "It's all this free-floating air up here. It makes me dizzy. It's a rush, actually, but I don't much care for it."

Quickly, then, Hercules told him what he had learned from the stable hand about the disappearances among those chosen to be summer queen, explaining that although the official explanation—they had gone off to seek their fortunes in the larger cities—was reasonable enough, it didn't explain the recent discovery of the remains of one woman.

Since he didn't think Demeter, being of the land and the seasons, had anything to do with it, he—

"You thought I did," Poseidon finished. His face darkened. The tips of the trident began to glow.

"I thought you might," Hercules corrected hastily. "*Might* know what's going on is what I meant."

They were a few hundred yards from the rocks Holix called dragon's teeth. From the distance the rocks appeared as vague shapes, despite the bright moon, and Hercules didn't much care for the shadows that lay between them. Or for the way his uncle stood, glaring at the water.

He waited for several minutes, knowing not to speak, knowing not to move.

"I am one of three," Poseidon said quietly, the glare fading to contemplation. "My brother Hades, my brother Zeus. We do not, and cannot, control each other, which is as it should be. We do not . . . we cannot control all that we oversee, which is, perhaps, not as it should be. Most, you understand, but not all."

Hercules moved to stand beside him.

The tide had turned.

"Klothon," his uncle said.

"What?"

"There is a creature out there, Hercules, called the Klothon." His free hand pointed along the horizon east to west. "It travels in the deepest parts of my kingdom, and beyond, where even I do not travel. It moves in a great circle, and so I'm fortunate not to have to see it more than once in a few years. A vicious beast. Evil." His chest rose slowly. "We have fought, too."

"You didn't win," Hercules ventured.

"Didn't lose either," Poseidon said. "If I had, my dear son Triton would be in charge, and I'd be sitting on a rock somewhere, writing stupid songs for the

102

Sirens.'' A grin, a quiet laugh. ''Not a bad life, actually, but my wife would kill me before I finished the first verse.''

Hercules knew that to be true enough. But if he let his uncle start talking about his family, it would be dawn before he'd hear the end of it. ''The Klothon?'' he prodded.

''It's here.''

That, Hercules thought glumly, is what I was afraid of.

Poseidon pointed at the promontory above the rocks. ''They'll put some poor child up there, thinking she's a real queen. By morning she'll be breakfast.''

''And you can't stop it?''

''I wish I could. I really do, Nephew. A lot of ships are lost out there, and not a few of them litter my place because of that *thing*.'' He faced Hercules then, and put a heavy hand on his shoulder. ''This is Hera's doing; you already know that. She wants you to be the hero you are and try to save the woman. She also knows that if I can't save her, it's not likely you'll be able to either. It's a death sentence, Hercules.''

That, Hercules thought, is also what I was afraid of.

''Does this Klothon have a weakness?''

Poseidon's hand dropped away. ''Are you kidding? It's a monster. Of course it has a weakness.''

Hercules blinked slowly. ''Then why haven't you used it against it?''

The sea god made a long low noise, expressing the kind of *for heaven's sake do I have to explain everything?* patience an elder has to dredge up in order to

103

deal with a young one who insists on acting dense.

Hercules stared at him.

Poseidon stared back.

Hercules wondered if his uncle had gone to the same teaching school as his mother; they both used the same method of silent staring to make him think, and make his life miserable.

Until, that is, Poseidon grinned. "This isn't the Klothon's element." He stamped a foot on the sand. "It's more at home in the water, right?"

Poseidon smiled: patience rewarded, though in this case the younger not the elder had dredged it up.

"Quicker in the water, slower on land," Hercules suggested.

Poseidon nodded. "Maybe slow enough for you to notice that there is quite a long but narrow area under its chin and running down toward its belly, an area that could definitely be pierced."

Hercules brightened. "And if I should pierce it?"

"Enough meat to feed that city for a hundred years." Poseidon winked. "And really tick Hera off. Unfortunately," he added, "you'd have be to quick as Hermes to pull it off. Assuming you could get at it in the first place. Assuming it really is that much slower on land. Assuming—"

"Enough, please," Hercules said. This was more than he had dared hope for, though less than he'd have liked—which was that Poseidon himself would do the honors and leave him, Hercules, out of it. Preferably a couple of miles inland.

Still, this was more information than he had when he'd arrived.

Now he just had to figure out what to do with it.

That's when he realized that Poseidon was already wading into the ocean.

"Thanks, Uncle," he called.

The trident waved, and a wave suddenly rose over Hercules' head, broke, and slammed him to his knees, sputtering.

Poseidon turned. "Oh. Sorry. Wasn't thinking."

Hercules could only nod; there still seemed to be a lake of saltwater in his mouth. He spat it out, wiped his face, and rose shakily, warily.

The sea was blank.

Nothing left but the moon and the tide.

And a large serpentine shadow that watched him from the moon's shimmering trail on the water.

12

Iolaus had no complaints about the rooms at the Red Boar. To be sure, they were small, but they were also fastidiously clean. Each had a single wide bed with a low table beside it, a chair, a woven hanging on the wall for color—utilitarian and comfortable, made for sleeping and not much else. A small window over-looked the boulevard, perfect for watching the parades and the pedestrians.

What he wasn't so sure about was Orena, the inn-keeper's wife, who insisted on accompanying him personally upstairs. Just to be sure, she explained, that he and his legendary companion would be satisfied with the accommodations. She was a pleasant-looking woman, although a shade too rotund for his taste, and loud, and he would have attributed her obsequious manner to a desire to prove to the council that the Red Boar knew how to handle visiting dignitaries had it not been for the way she kept bumping into him with her not inconsiderable hips.

Constantly.

And batting her blue-painted eyes.

Not to mention the giggling and the waggling of her thick eyebrows and the way her hands almost but not quite touched him whenever she spoke, or giggled, or batted her eyes.

It drove him crazy.

Yet he couldn't bring himself to be rude, and so he endured the clumsy flirtations until, at last, he managed to convince her that everything was absolutely wonderful, that the council would be fully informed of the wonders of the Red Boar Inn, and that he really did need a few minutes alone.

"To rest," he added with a courteous smile. "It's been a long day."

Orena giggled, almost touched him, and batted her eyelids so rapidly the wind nearly put the bedside candle out. "Well, when you've done," she said breathily, "come downstairs. There'll be a meal and drink for you. And your friend, when he gets back." The eyelids batted again. "On the house, naturally. Your money's no good as long as you stay here."

He thanked her profusely as he eased her into the hallway, then closed the door and sagged gratefully against it. Somehow the room now felt remarkably like a prison. It didn't take long to figure out that the chair wouldn't hold the door against a determined pusher, but the window was at least large enough for him to wriggle through if he had to.

"Brother," he whispered, and dumped his travel sack onto the bed. He sat for a minute, scratching his head vigorously, wondering what Herc was up to. If he knew his friend at all, it had something to do with

107

Holix's story, and the kid's red-faced admission that he was head over heels for a rich man's servant.

Iolaus grinned—a twin, no less.

Some guys had all the luck.

Nevertheless, that was something he would worry about in the morning. Right now he was hungry, he was thirsty, and by checking out the other inns in the area, he just might learn a few things. About the festival. About the missing women. And even perhaps about those ridiculous rebels.

Five minutes saw him changed into a plain leather vest and snug black pants with matching boots, a dagger in his belt, and his sword shoved under the bed. A minute after that he was downstairs in the inn's main room, taking in the tantalizing aromas of good food and wine. Every table was occupied, the conversation close to boisterous, but he didn't mind. He stood at the bar, accepted a full goblet from a giggling Orena, and leaned back to see whom he might join to hear a little gossip.

That didn't take long, either.

Luck had decided to bless him tonight.

In the back corner was a table for four. Three women without escorts were seated around it, and as he watched he noticed how easily they fended off the occasional man who attempted to join them. Unlike the rest of the room, they were definitely not in a party mood.

He sipped, waited, and finally made his way over.

The women looked up, scowling and muttering.

Iolaus simply smiled.

"Well, well, well," he said pleasantly. "Mind if I sit down, Venitia?"

She was gorgeous.

Gone was the eye patch and tatty rebel clothes, replaced by a dress that was, he thought happily, just this side of being labeled illegal. Her blond hair was brushed back from her ears and fell in curly waves to the middle of her spine. Around her throat she wore a necklace of shells and false gems, and on her left wrist was a simple, thin gold bracelet.

He didn't wait for her answer; by the stunned look on her face, it would have taken forever anyway. He dragged a chair over and sat to her left, toasted them all with his goblet, and watched them carefully as he drank. The woman on his left—short dark hair, tiny dark eyes, very thin, a dress the cousin of Venitia's— avoided his gaze by tracing the tabletop's grain with her thumb; the woman opposite him—long black hair braided around her skull, green eyes, a high-necked dress trimmed in white fur—only nodded to him stiffly, her thin lips drawn tight.

"What do you want?" Venitia at last demanded hoarsely.

He set the goblet down. "I don't know. A pleasant meal. Pleasant company. A few answers to some silly questions. Nothing much."

"Silly questions?" She leaned close, eyes narrowed. "What silly questions?"

"Gee, I don't know," he said again. "Like . . . oh . . . I don't know . . . like, what in the gods' names are you three doing in here when half the city guards are hunting for you to throw you into prison for the rest of your lives, if they don't draw and quarter you first and feed you to the fish? Are you out of your damn minds?'' He shrugged. ''Like that.''

Venitia blinked so rapidly, Iolaus was reminded of Orena. He shuddered, and drank quickly before he did something stupid.

''Well?'' he asked mildly.

''We don't have to talk to you,'' said the short-haired woman.

''Oh, hush, Bea,'' Venitia said without looking at her. ''He probably knows already anyway.''

Bea closed her eyes in resignation. ''Nuts.''

''We could kill him,'' the third woman suggested. ''Who'd know? Who'd care?''

''He's a judge, Zarel,'' Venitia snapped in disgust. ''Use your head, okay?''

Bea recommended leaving immediately.

Zarel figured they could kill him and no one would notice because the city would be on fire from the rebel attack in the morning, so who'd care anyway.

Iolaus picked up his goblet again, realized it was empty, and waved it over his head. In seconds a barmaid hovered at the table, ignoring the complaints of those patrons who'd been waiting forever for her attention.

''Have you eaten?'' he asked the three women. He could tell from their expressions that they had not, and so he ordered meals all around, wine all around, and would have gone so far as to suggest a private room had he not abruptly remembered Zarel's unnerving blood lust.

110

This will do just as well, he decided. For one thing, there were plenty of witnesses.

When the barmaid left, Venitia leaned close again. "Don't think this puts us in your debt, you scum."

"Don't do that," he said, staring at her forehead.

She frowned. "Do what?"

"What you're doing."

Her frown deepened. "What am I doing?"

He tried to pantomime the disconcerting effect her leaning forward produced, smiled weakly, and finally made a point to stare hard and briefly at her cleavage.

Bea giggled.

Zarel said, "Pig," and rolled her eyes in revulsion.

Once she understood, Venitia blushed so vividly her freckles vanished and he thought she would pass out. But she did sit up while her hands fluttered to her chest, flew away, fluttered back, dropped to the table, fluttered back, and finally dove into her lap, where they clenched each other until her knuckles turned white.

For his part, Iolaus made a great show of waiting for the barmaid, practically leaping to his feet in relief when she returned with plates heaped with bread and steaming food. "Be my guest," he said expansively.

When they didn't move, he sat and added, "The council's paying for it."

The magic words.

They ate, they drank, and they ignored him completely until at last he tapped Venitia on the shoulder.

"What?" she said, practically yelling.

Keeping his voice as friendly as possible, he said, "No offense, but you're all fakes, aren't you? This

111

rebel stuff is a crock." When they rose as one to leave, he tightened his voice and said, "Sit. Down."

They did.

Then he folded his arms on the table and lowered his head slightly to indicate a conversation not meant to be overheard. To their credit, they didn't argue.

"You can claim these clothes are disguises," he said, "but they're not; you're too used to them. I'm guessing it's the other way around, right?"

No answers; he didn't need them.

"I'm also guessing that you're not really rebels, and there'll be no attack in the morning. I mean"—he raised his voice to cut off Zarel's heated protest—"not in the sense that you're out to overthrow the government, burn the city down, and make life better for all those poor, oppressed peasants I saw dancing in the streets today. What I don't know is why."

"Guess," Zarel sneered.

Bea sighed. "You're right," she confessed.

"Oh, great." Zarel sat back angrily and folded her arms across her chest. "Just great."

"But he knows," Bea protested.

"He didn't know, you stupid cow. He was guessing!"

"Well, he said he was guessing, but he wasn't. Not really. He was more thinking out loud, kind of. Wondering, you know?"

Zarel closed her eyes.

Venitia, who hadn't taken her gaze off Iolaus' face, squeaked, "Are you married?"

"Gods and demons!" Zarel exploded. She jumped to her feet, her hands in fists. "Are you two crazy?

112

Don't you see what he's doing? Don't . . . don't . . . oh, the hell with it.'' With a look that demanded they follow without question, she stomped out of the inn, although not before decking a drunk who tried to paw at her behind.

Bea rose more slowly. "I'm sorry," she said. "She has a temper, you know? It's like a thing with her, you see. A flaw. I'd better go with her; otherwise she'll cut someone's throat and it'll take hours to get her out of jail again.''

Iolaus waited until they were alone before he looked at Venitia. "Again?"

"You're not married?"

"That woman has killed people before?" Iolaus asked.

Venitia looked crestfallen. "Oh. You are married."

I'm in one of Herc's dreams, he thought wildly; that's what this is—a Hercules dream.

He forced himself to breathe deeply and slowly several times. Then he took Venitia's hands in his and squeezed them just enough to make her shake her head. And smile.

"Sorry," she said. "I don't know what got into me."

"It's my curse and my charm," he told her.

She laughed, and didn't pull away. "Yes."

"Yes what?"

"Yes, she has killed before, but her father's so rich, it doesn't matter as long as she does it to someone who doesn't matter. And you're right about us." She hesitated, moistening her lips nervously. "I . . . I'm not sure."

113

"Look," he said, holding up a finger, "Hercules and I already know you're not rebels, so you're not talking out of turn. Believe me, we've been up against the real thing more times than I care to remember. But," he added when he noticed the distressed look on her face, "we're not going to turn you in, either. We also know something's not right around here, and if you need help, we'll be glad to give it."

She touched his nose with a finger. "You're cute."

Oh, boy, he thought; oh . . . boy.

"It's a short story, though," she said.

And leaned toward him.

Without blushing.

Iolaus swallowed. "Stretch it," he suggested. "I've got all night."

Her gaze wandered over his face while her expression told him that she was inwardly debating. A moral dilemma. When she finally made her decision, she did so with a deep breath that had him gasping once, blinking twice, and reaching hastily for his goblet.

"I'm going to tell you about Klothon," she announced.

Iolaus was baffled. "What? Who's that?"

"Not a who. It's a what."

"What?"

She nodded.

He took a drink, lifted a finger, and said, carefully, "What?"

"Yes."

"Yes . . . what?"

She frowned. "Right. What."

"What what?"

"Huh?"

He took another drink. A long one this time, and waved the goblet for a refill. While he waited he ran through the conversation again, as slowly as he could. Without looking at her.

It worked.

"Klothon isn't a who," he concluded. "It's a what."

"That's what I said."

"Okay. And what, exactly, is it?"

"Well, for one thing, if you don't leave before the queen is crowned, it's the thing that's going to kill you."

13

Hercules woke to the sound of laughter in the street, and the distant heralding of trumpets. For a second he could not recall where he was, could recall only the night spent by the ocean. When he did at last get his bearings, he sat up with a muffled groan, rubbed his eyes, looked around the room blearily, and nearly fell back again when he saw someone slumped in his chair.

Iolaus, his eyes closed, moaned, hands pressed to his head, legs outstretched.

"Good morning," Hercules said as he reached his arms over his head.

"Don't yell. I can hear you."

Hercules lowered his voice, but couldn't help a grin. "Hard night?"

Iolaus nodded, moaned, and let one hand fall wearily to the armrest. His eyes didn't open. "I spent practically the whole night here. All in the line of duty, I want you to know."

"I'm sure it was."

Iolaus grunted, knowing his friend didn't believe him. "As a matter of fact, while you were out doing . . . whatever . . . I was talking to some of our so-called rebels. The three women we saw in the cave."

Hercules lifted an eyebrow. "Really?"

Iolaus made a face. "Yes. Really. You want to know what I found out?"

Hercules stretched again and yawned loudly. "Sure, why not?"

"Well, for one thing, they're not really rebels."

Hercules nodded. "We figured that one right."

"Yeah, but what we didn't figure is that they're being paid by someone to make trouble. It isn't much, but they're not rich. They could use the dinars. Venitia doesn't know who the money man is, but that Rotus guy probably does since he's the one who hands it out."

Hercules wasn't really surprised. From what the fake rebels and Holix had said, he already suspected Titus Perical was somehow behind it. Stirring up the political pot, he pointed out, was an easy way to stay in power until he didn't want to stay in power any longer. Especially since he didn't seem to be that terrible a ruler.

"That's what she said," Iolaus confirmed. "Do you have any idea how much wine a little woman like that can drink?"

"Nope."

"It's disgusting. It was all I could do to keep up with her."

Hercules pushed back on the bed and leaned against the wall, the window over his left shoulder. Street

117

sounds increased as the city continued to awaken, and the tinted light slipping into the room told him there was probably haze in the sky. Iolaus, however, was too hungover to notice much of anything. It figured that with the entire rebel band undoubtedly roaming the city, he would be the one to happen upon the women. It also figured that with his kind of luck, they would be able to outlast him in a drinking contest. Based on the way the poor guy looked, it was a miracle he was able to breathe, much less sit up without falling over.

Nevertheless, Hercules said, "You did well."

"Say that in my eulogy." Iolaus moaned louder and winced. "By the way, she also said there's a monster around."

"Klothon."

Iolaus opened one eye. "You know?"

Hercules nodded, and described his visit with Poseidon, although he managed to leave out the dunking part at the end. Iolaus wouldn't have forgotten it, and wouldn't have let him forget it, either.

The eye closed. "Damn. I could have saved myself some trouble."

Hercules laughed. "Oh, right. A lot of trouble you went to."

"I did, Herc! You have no idea what it was like, interrogating that woman. She's very clever, you know. Sneaky. I had to use every trick in the book to learn what I did." He sighed. "Maybe she'll come to my funeral."

"There will be a funeral, a double one, if I don't get something to eat soon. I've starving, and we have a full day ahead of us."

So saying, he got up, hauled a protesting Iolaus to his feet, and got them both downstairs for a breakfast he made sure was as large as he could eat, just to watch his friend squirm. Iolaus only drank water, and managed a few bites of bread.

Afterward they stood in front of the inn, watching the pedestrians stream leisurely toward the plaza. Bright clothing was the order of the day, no matter what the station of the wearer. Slow-moving chariots festooned with feathers and ribbons pressed down the boulevard's center, joined by carts and wagons similarly outfitted. The horses were also festively decked out for the occasion—manes and tails were braided and wound through with gold and silver threads; some horses wore standing plumes between their ears, and one had a depiction of Mount Olympus painted on its flank.

The sidelines weren't immune to the festivities, either, as merchants hawked their wares in front of their shops, offering everything from rare antique statues of Demeter and Poseidon to tiny rugs handwoven by goddess-blessed maidens who lived alone in the mountains and never saw the light of day.

It was a street of scams and chaos, but no one seemed to mind.

"I'm going deaf," Iolaus complained in the din.

Hercules gave him a sympathetic nudge, although he noticed that his friend wasn't so far in his grave that he didn't glance lasciviously at many of the ladies parading by.

"Now what?" Iolaus rubbed his hands together, his hangover seemingly cured by the excitement and bustle of the festival.

They weren't expected until the ceremonial banquet at sunset, the judging to follow, but the temptation to join the plaza throng was powerful. It would be, Hercules admitted, a fine way to spend the day: watching acrobats and trained animals, listening to music, sampling good food until they were ready to burst. Or they could go down to the harbor and do the same thing, this time with a nautical twist.

"I vote for the plaza," Iolaus answered quickly. "The water reminds me there's that Klothon thing out there. I'll want to *eat* lunch, not *be* lunch."

Hercules shook his head. When Iolaus didn't argue, something had to be wrong. "Something the matter?"

Iolaus passed a hand over his face. "No. Well . . . no. It's just that I seem to remember Venitia telling me something I should remember to tell you, but I can't remember what she said it was."

Hercules sounded dubious. "If there was anything at all, that is."

"Yeah." Iolaus nodded. "That's the problem."

"It'll come to you," Hercules told him. "Let's go."

"The plaza?"

"The stables."

"Oh, sure, that was easily my third choice. Nothing like the bracing aroma of manure first thing in the morning. Best cure for a hangover." He scowled. "Either you're trying to kill me, or teach me a lesson, right?"

For an answer Hercules gave his shoulder a gentle shove, and they stepped into the crowd. While they walked to the stables he explained that he wanted to have another talk with Holix. Although Iolaus didn't see the reason for it, he didn't object. His head was still throbbing, his legs felt like rubber stilts, and the thought of facing an entire city population crammed into one space was more than he could handle.

It would probably kill him, he asserted.

Hercules laughed heartily, much to Iolaus' chagrin, and then asked if Iolaus had figured out how they were going to deal with the dilemma of having both to pick and not pick a queen that night.

Iolaus stared at him, baffled.

Hercules explained. "If we pick someone, she dies, Iolaus. Therefore we shouldn't pick any of the contestants. But then how are we going to *not* pick anyone and still make sure the festival isn't ruined?"

Iolaus thought about that one for a while. "You got it all wrong, Herc, though it doesn't much matter in the end."

Now it was Hercules' turn to look baffled. "Come again?"

Iolaus sighed with the effort of thinking. "How are we going to pick one when, according to the kid, Titus has already decided on the winner? You don't think he's going to try to bribe us, do you?"

They swerved around a pair of well-dressed, corpulent men arguing in the middle of the street. Each stood in a garishly decorated chariot drawn by horses who looked to Hercules to be glad for the respite. A crowd had begun to gather around them, suggesting possible epithets and curses for the men to hurl at each other. There was, for the moment, more laughter than anger.

The stable's alley was just beyond, and when Hercules and Iolaus broke free of the crowd, Hercules glanced skyward and said, "Maybe we'll get lucky."

As he had thought, a haze covered the sky's usual sharp blue, the sun a distant smear of faded gold.

Iolaus followed his gaze, and frowned. "Hercules, no offense, but I don't think any rain is going to stop this ceremony. It's too important to these people."

"Wishful thinking, my friend, just wishful thinking."

The stable seemed empty as they approached it, which Hercules thought was odd. Holix had told him that all the serious training was done at a facility near the city's outskirts, but that the horses would be brought here before dawn, to get them ready for the parades. But he saw no chariots or decorated wagons, and except for those who passed the alley's far end, he saw no people either.

No windows in the facing walls, scattered piles of discarded planks and garbage thrown at their base. Although the surrounding rooftops didn't overhang the narrow passage, still the light seemed dimmer, less friendly.

Iolaus stopped. "Herc."

Hercules stopped as well. They were some twenty yards from the open stable doors, and he couldn't help feeling that despite appearances, the building wasn't empty. "What?"

Turning to face the boulevard, he squinted at the crowd still surrounding the arguing charioteers. "I think I remember now what it was that Venitia said."

A tall man moved out of the stable's shadows, and there was movement behind him.

Hercules nodded absently.

Rotus wore no mask this time, but he did wear studded leather armor, and was carrying a short sword as if he knew how to use it. For that matter, Hercules thought with a *how the hell do I get into these things?* sigh, so did the eight men who stepped into the light behind him.

Oblivious to the threat, Iolaus continued: "I think she said some of them weren't kidding this year."

"Iolaus, turn around," Hercules muttered fiercely

Iolaus complied. "Oh" was all he said. He rubbed a nervous palm over his chest. "This isn't going to be fun, Herc. Four-to-one is lousy odds."

Hercules would have agreed, and would not have objected if Iolaus had suggested they beat a sane if hasty retreat, had not someone inside the stable chosen that particular moment to toss Holix into the alley. There was blood on the young man's tunic, and even at this distance, Hercules could see that his face was cut and bruised.

"Holix," he called, "are you all right?"

With an effort the young man lifted his head and squinted through puffy eyes. "Hercules?"

"Yes."

"So do I look all right?"

Hercules knew it had been a stupid question, but he wanted to make sure the kid was still alive.

Iolaus began to back away then, even as his hand covered the hilt of his sword. "I know what you're thinking, Herc, and it's a bad idea. I think we ought to find someplace safe, think this over, come up with a plan and—*whoop!*" he suddenly cried when Hercules reached back without turning, snared his shoulder, and yanked him back to his side.

"I'm not going to leave him."

Iolaus blew out a breath. "I didn't think so. Okay, so what do we do? The straightforward charge, the divide-and-conquer, the leap-over-their-heads-and-come-down-on-the-other-side, or what?"

At that moment Rotus nodded sharply.

The rebels charged.

"Whatever," Hercules said, and braced himself.

As he watched the upraised swords he knew that Iolaus had been right.

This wasn't going to be any fun at all.

14

Unlike the last time, Rotus' men were obviously out for blood, yet Hercules and Iolaus at least had the advantage of the alley's narrow width. By standing only a yard apart, they were able to prevent the others from sneaking around behind them.

Unfortunately it didn't prevent the swords the others wielded from taking vicious swipes at various exposed limbs, heads, and far too many vital organs for Hercules' peace of mind.

What did help was his reputation.

In spite of Rotus' exhortations—as usual, shouted from the safety of the rear of the fray—the rebels were tentative in their attack after their initial run brought them face-to-face with their intended victims. This allowed Hercules to sidestep a clumsy thrust, trap the man's arm against his side with his own arm, and bring a heavy fist down on his skull. Before the man could fall, Hercules picked him up by arm and waist and tossed him into the others, spilling at least half of them to the ground.

At the same time Iolaus faced a wildly determined man who used his weapon like a bat, swinging it two-handed and so rapidly that Iolaus was barely able to parry each blow. Forced to give reluctant ground, he ducked one swing, sucked in his stomach to avoid another, and very nearly lost his own weapon when a third slash stung his arms to the shoulders and made him gasp.

Luckily the collision rattled the attacker as well, and in the slight hesitation that ensued, Iolaus spun in a complete circle for added power and brought the flat of his blade solidly against the man's side, propelling him off balance to his left.

The wall took care of the rest when skull met stone.

"There's only two of them, you fools!" Rotus yelled.

"Don't see you getting all sweaty," one of his men snapped just before Hercules grabbed him by the throat, lifted him off his feet, and shook him so hard his helmet fell off, his sword dropped to the alley floor, and his eyes crossed.

Iolaus laughed, grabbed the sword of the rebel now slumped against the base of the wall, and turned just as two others rushed him. Although he would have rather had a lighter weapon in his left hand, he managed to keep both of them at bay long enough for him to figure out that as long as he didn't slip or slide, he might last long enough for Hercules to lend a hand.

But when the man on his right lunged at the same time as his companion swung, Iolaus couldn't move his own swords fast enough. One enemy blade was blocked, but the other caught him square on the hip.

He yelped, went down on one knee, and got both hands up just in time to form a shaky X, in whose crotch the other blades slammed home.

It was a test of strength: could they force him onto his back before he was able to regain his feet?

Sweat broke along his brow and slid into his eyes, stinging and blurring his vision.

"Going to die, friend," one of them grunted.

"Herc!" Iolaus called.

The other rebel laughed, and pushed harder.

Hercules had to make a choice—there was a trio of rebels trying to slip around his flank, whom he could thwart by tossing the man currently in his hands at them, or he could toss the man in hand at the men who had Iolaus in hand.

No real choice at all.

"Fly," he whispered.

A second later Iolaus spotted something flying in the air between the heads of the two straining rebels, and braced his feet when he recognized the terrified expression of a third, who seemed awfully red in the face as he hurtled through space. When the collision occurred, Iolaus shoved himself backward and would have escaped completely had not the flying man slightly overshot his companions.

Helmet met jaw, and the last thing Iolaus saw was either his soul on its way to Hades or a hell of a gorgeous cloud floating over Themon.

Hercules, on the other hand, saw nothing but a tangle of thrashing limbs and swords.

He did, however, feel the weight of three men land-ing on his back, bending him double as they flailed wildly whatever they could flail, except their swords, which they dropped immediately once they realized that by flailing them they were likely to puncture each other.

Hercules managed to drag one of them around to the ground, then propel himself up and back as fast as he could. When the ungainly pile hit the wall, Hercules staggered forward, using his right hand to stop himself from falling.

A quick step, and he was standing upright; a quick turn, and his hands were ready for whatever they'd come up with next.

He didn't count on the plank Rotus carried.

Well, damn, he thought just before it smacked him.

Stunned, he dropped heavily onto his rump, hands out behind him.

He wanted desperately to get back on his feet, but nothing seemed to work except his eyes, and they were letting in far too much light. Yet, paradoxically, he felt blinded, even though he could see swift-moving shadows through the sudden glare; his ears rang, even though he thought he heard voices raised in alarm; and when his right arm finally gave way, the fall to the ground seemed to take forever.

Once he hit, instinct brought up his right arm for protection against whatever Rotus had in mind for an encore. When nothing happened, he felt his brain throb with bewilderment.

That was when an arm eased around his shoulders and helped him to sit up.

"You okay?"

He blinked, squinted, blinked again several times,

and tried to clear his head by shaking it, although not so hard that it fell off.

"I'll get some water," said whoever was holding him

"Thanks," he said.

That he felt foolish was an understatement.

That he couldn't deny the anger that tightened his jaw made him almost as upset as feeling foolish.

Anger sometimes made him forget just how powerful he was.

He inhaled slowly, deeply, several times, and started when a hand cupped the back of his head while another held a bowl of water to his lips. He drank gratefully, the cool liquid soon reviving him enough to be able to look into the face of a dark-haired woman without getting dizzy.

"Bea," she said with a shy smile.

"Thank you, Bea." He frowned. "Iolaus?"

There was no need for a reply. He spotted his friend on the ground a few feet away, a lovely blonde leaning over him. "It's all right, Herc," Iolaus called weakly. "I'm just going over my funeral arrangements."

Hercules grinned and, with Bea's nervous help, got back to his feet.

The rebels were gone, and at either end of the alley he could see groups of people staring and whispering.

Then he saw Holix.

The young man lay where he had been thrown, conscious now and groaning. Hercules hurried to his side and looked him over. Although there was a frightening amount of blood, most of it seemed to come from a wound beneath his hair. His eyes were puffed closed, and his lower lip was split.

Anger rose again.

"Iolaus, get up." Hercules scooped Holix easily into his arms. "We're going back to the inn."

Iolaus didn't argue. He did, however, take his time standing, and seemed to lean rather heavily against the woman whose offer of assistance he accepted with a feeble and somewhat overdramatic nod.

Hercules paused when he reached them. It took a moment to place the woman. The last time he had seen her, she had worn an eye patch. "Venitia?" he inquired.

After scooting around to Iolaus' other side, she nodded.

"He's faking," Hercules told her with a brief smile and a wink.

"Hey!" Iolaus protested. "I'm wounded here."

"So is Holix, and he's not in good shape." He turned to Bea. "Will you come with us?"

"Yes."

"Can I trust you?"

She looked shocked. "Of course!"

"Sorry, but things are a little confusing around here today."

A tentative smile was her acceptance of the apology, and he hurried off, cradling Holix against his jarring strides as best he could. The crowd at the alley's mouth parted quickly, and it took only a few minutes to reach the Red Boar. As soon as he walked in, Orena lumbered over from behind the bar, demanded an explanation, and without waiting to receive one, preceded them up the stairs to Hercules' room.

"On the bed," she ordered. When Holix was down, she knelt on the floor beside him and grunted. "Took a good one in the chops here." Deft fingers parted the blood-and-grime-matted hair. "Gods, this is ugly. Not bad, though."

Hercules hovered at the foot of the bed, not smiling at all when she scowled at him.

"This is an inn," she told him brusquely. "I get more busted heads and broken bones than you can shake a sheep at." Finally she smiled. "I can fix him up, don't worry." With that, she ordered Bea and Venitia down to the kitchen for hot water and clean rags, pulled out a knife tucked into her rope girdle, and began to slice the tunic away from Holix's chest. "How's the little guy?"

"Hey!" Iolaus protested from the chair where Venitia had left him. And frowned when he realized he'd been saying that a lot. "I'm fine," he added grumpily, and touched his jaw gingerly. "No thanks to Hercules."

Hercules swung his head around. "What?"

"You threw that guy too far," Iolaus complained.

"I was in a hurry, if you remember."

"I could have handled them, you know."

"You called for help."

"I—"

"Boys!" Orena snapped with a laugh. "Do you mind?"

"Yeah," Holix muttered. And went rigid when the innkeeper prodded his ribs with gentle fingers.

"You're the horse trainer, aren't you?" she asked, brushing some hair out of his eyes.

"Yes."

"You ride in the parade?"

"I hope so."

"Wear a mask," she suggested. "You'll scare the children."

Holix tried to laugh, coughed, moaned, and passed out.

Orena settled back on her heels and dusted her palms against her chest. "That's better. Easier to work on when they're unconscious."

It was obvious that she wanted them to leave. Hercules jerked his head toward the door, and Iolaus followed him into the narrow passageway.

"What happened?"

Iolaus pushed his hands back through his hair. "Some people saw the fight and started yelling, Venitia said. Rotus took off."

"We were lucky."

Iolaus touched his chin. "Speak for yourself." He glanced at the doorway. "You think that's Hera's doing?"

"No. This is something else. A complication."

"Of course. There's always a complication. Easy, Herc, is not the way you live your life."

"Maybe, maybe not." Hercules' expression hardened. "But there are things we have to check on before tonight. There has to be a way to keep Holix's girl from . . ." He didn't have to finish.

"Things to check on," Iolaus echoed glumly. "We checked on Holix, and nearly got sliced. If you want to check the city, we'll probably blow it up.''

Hercules grinned, slapped his friend's shoulder, and hurried off to meet Bea and Venitia in the main room. He asked them to keep an eye on Holix.

"Where are you going?'' Venitia asked Iolaus.

"To the crowning site,'' Hercules answered.

"You'll need a guide,'' she told Iolaus.

"We'll need a guide,'' Iolaus agreed.

"I've been near there,'' Hercules said. "I think I can find the way.''

"She might know a shortcut,'' Iolaus suggested hopefully. "And after what we've been through, it could help.''

"I know a shortcut,'' Venitia volunteered.

Hercules looked from one to the other, and from the corner of his eye didn't miss the knowing grin on Bea's face. Taking the hint a few beats late, she offered to watch Holix herself. With Orena around, she added, she didn't think Rotus would try anything. Before Hercules could argue, she also suggested a message be sent to Holix's girl; it wouldn't be all that difficult to learn where she lived.

"Settled,'' Iolaus proclaimed with a clap. "Nothing to it once you get organized.''

Before Hercules realized what had happened, Iolaus and Venitia had hustled him into the street, where he listened with growing alarm to the directions she gave to the crowning site. He'd have to be blind and blind stupid not to know she wanted to spend as much time with Iolaus as she could, but time was short, and none of it could be wasted on dalliance with females. There were lives at stake.

He cleared his throat as meaningfully as he could without actually adding a pop to Iolaus' head for emphasis.

"She's only kidding, Herc," he said. "We'll be there before you know it."

"I was only kidding," Venitia agreed. "Follow me. It won't take long."

"Okay," Hercules said. "But take it easy." A tilt of his head indicated the crowds the boulevard held.

Iolaus didn't miss it.

With that number of people in robes, cloaks, and voluminous fancy dress, it would be easy to hide a dagger, or a sword, until the last moment.

This time there would be no warning.

And nothing they could do to stop it.

15

By the time they reached the site, Hercules was ready to climb the nearest wall, or go headfirst down the cliff without bothering with a rope.

It wasn't the route; that had been fine. Venitia had led them through streets and alleys she knew wouldn't be jammed with people, and it wasn't long before they were standing under the wall of trees.

Neither was it the increasingly complicated problems they faced. That part was easy—Hercules simply decided to stop thinking about their problems, because he knew that whatever their solutions, they wouldn't materialize until the moment was right. And by thinking about them as much as he had been, he took his attention away from his immediate surroundings.

No, it wasn't the route and it wasn't his complicated problems. It was Venitia.

Every so often she would drop back from Iolaus' side and ask, "Is he married?"

"No," he'd answered the first time.

She had grinned, blushed, and rushed to catch up.

The second time, he'd answered "No" with a shrug that he had hoped would tell her Iolaus wasn't looking to *get* married, either, and she was wasting her time.

The third time, he just said "No."

The fourth time, he grunted.

After that, he couldn't remember doing anything except giving her looks that would have fried someone less determined than she.

It would be impossible to count the number of times he had witnessed the astonishing effect his friend had on women. They either passed him off as a decent-looking kind of short guy who happened to be Hercules' traveling buddy—a reaction that irked Iolaus to no end and produced a lot of grumbling tirades—or the lust flame was turned so high, it scorched half the countryside—a reaction that usually turned Iolaus' brain to mush.

Venitia, however, was in a class by herself.

This, Hercules reckoned with a mixture of amusement and mild alarm, wasn't merely a reaction to Iolaus and his charm, it was the onset of an all-out matrimonial campaign.

"Doesn't look like much, does it?" Iolaus commented when they arrived, leaning against a gray-barked tree, arms folded loosely over his chest.

Hercules agreed.

The site was a simple open area of low grass that led to the edge of a seaward cliff. Far to his right Hercules could see the fishing community at the east end of the bay; to the left nothing but sand and wind-blown plain.

There was no decoration, no shrine, no indication at all that this was a special place.

Venitia lowered herself to the ground, shivering slightly.

Although the sun still shone brightly, its effect had been muted by the deepening haze. The light wind that blew in off the water brought with it a faint chill, making it feel more like twilight than the middle of the day.

"Wait here," Hercules told them, and stepped away from the trees.

"Are you sure you're not married?" he heard Venitia ask.

He didn't hear Iolaus' answer; he only heard the wind as it swept his hair away from his face and made him squint at the pricks of light that sparked across the water.

At the edge he looked down.

Fifty or sixty feet, he estimated; maybe a little less, maybe a little more.

The line of boulders he had seen the night before with Poseidon was far more imposing now when seen from above. Gulls squatted on some, their feathers puffed against the chill, but each of the tall rocks had a narrow bladelike top, too narrow even for the birds to use with any degree of comfort. He couldn't help thinking of some great beast that had lunged out of the water and buried itself into the cliffside; what was left exposed were the jagged bones of its tail.

He wondered about the Klothon.

Poseidon had conveniently not described it, and

from what he understood from Holix and Venitia, no one on land had ever seen it.

And lived, that is.

What sort of beast could rear itself this high out of the sea, grab a victim, and vanish again, all without leaving a trace?

He passed a hand over his chest, deciding that he really didn't want to know.

A large bird coasted overhead, its shadow brief and chilly.

He checked the sky again, this time letting his senses do the work for him, senses that weren't necessarily restricted to his eyes and ears.

He let the presence of the sea touch him; he felt the wind and all the wind carried on it; the weight of the sky; the smell of the air.

He sensed Iolaus standing beside him, but the man said nothing; he knew what Hercules was after.

Finally Hercules shook himself and glanced at his friend. "Hera" was all he said.

Iolaus frowned. "Where?"

"I don't know. Near." He gestured toward the horizon. "There's going to be a storm."

"I know that already. Just look at the sky."

"No. Something . . ." Hercules' eyes narrowed as he searched for the right word; then he shook his head in frustration. "Something more, I think. I'm not sure."

Iolaus rubbed the side of his neck thoughtfully before shrugging. "Can't help you, Herc."

"That's okay. Just know that it's Hera. How, I don't know, but it is."

He beckoned Venitia to him. She obeyed apprehensively, as if she believed he still didn't quite trust her. If that was the case, she was right. It had nothing to do with her infatuation with Iolaus; it had everything to do with her convenient appearance in the alley that morning. Although Hercules doubted that she was part of Rotus' still-unknown plans, he couldn't for the life of him figure out why she was with the rebels in the first place.

Rebels weren't always a type, but if there was one, she wasn't it.

"Themon," he said, turning to face the city. The half mile between the gentle drop to the sand and the first of the buildings was unbroken by trees or large rocks. "Why does it sit back there, and the fishermen stay over there?"

"The sea," Venitia answered, and explained how the sea had battered the original village, and how the original villagers decided that swimming wasn't as much fun as they used to think. "Sometimes," she said, "we get a really bad winter storm, and the waves slide right up the boulevard, because it's lower than the ground by a couple of feet. You can see that even from here. Sometimes the water almost gets into the city itself." She smiled. "My mother says that wouldn't be a bad thing. It would clean up the streets without anyone doing any work."

He looked at Themon's modest sprawl without responding, turned toward the sea, followed the swath of the boulevard-turned-road through the low grass to the sand. Maybe, he thought, the old city fathers had hoped Themon would eventually make its way back to the sea. It was a lot of work for a street that had no buildings along it.

He also figured the people had long memories, and the stories of new Themon's beginning hadn't faded.

"It's a nice place," he said absently, meaning it.

"Oh, I love it," Venitia answered eagerly. "I really do."

He glanced at her sideways, but she didn't notice. She had decided to point out to Iolaus the boats swarming on the water; even the festival couldn't stop the work.

The pride in her voice was unmistakable.

Suddenly he grinned.

Hercules laughed.

Bewildered, Iolaus looked at him. "Are you all right?"

"I'm fine," he said. "Something just clicked, that's all." He put an easy hand on Venitia's shoulder, gripping it gently when she flinched. It didn't take long before he knew he was right. "You're Titus' daughter, aren't you?"

"What?" Iolaus yelped. "Are you nuts, Herc? She can't be, she's a rebel!"

"Oh, yeah," he said quietly, without taking his gaze from the young woman's astonished, and abruptly flushed, face. "I'll bet she is."

"But you saw her!" Iolaus flapped his arms. "He saw you, right? In the cave, I mean. *I* saw you in the cave." He frowned. "You *were* in the cave, right? Eye patch and everything, right?"

She nodded, but she didn't look at him. The

140

ground, at that moment, had become inexplicably fascinating.

Iolaus continued talking as if to avoid realizing the truth of Hercules' words. "Well, there you go, then, Herc. She was in the cave."

Hercules nodded.

"She was . . ." Iolaus blinked. "She was . . ." He put a hand to his mouth, stared at Venitia as if he was seeing her for the first time, and rolled his eyes while he clapped a palm to his forehead. "I'm an idiot."

No one disagreed.

"You *could* say I'm not an idiot, you know," Iolaus grumbled.

"You're not an idiot," Hercules said obligingly, dropping his hand, shaking his head. "I just figured it out now."

"You guessed," his friend accused.

"I guessed," he admitted.

Iolaus nodded sharply. "It's the eyes, right?"

"The eyes. The mouth." Hercules laughed silently. "You are definitely your father's daughter."

Venitia shrugged. "I'm also a rotten rebel," she said, although her mouth trembled as if trying to fight off a smile. "He works so hard, he hardly pays any attention to Mother or me, so when I heard about Rotus, I volunteered, even though I really didn't know what the problem supposedly was." She giggled. "It didn't occur to me at the time that becoming a rebel wasn't going to get me noticed by my father, since I was wearing a disguise."

Iolaus stared at her in admiration. "Does your father suspect?"

"I still have my head," Venitia replied, "so I guess not."

Hercules touched her arm to get her attention. "You helped us in the alley."

She nodded; instant shyness.

"What happened? Between you and your friends, and Rotus."

She gazed at Themon for several long seconds, hugging herself against the chill of the breeze. "At first it was fun. At least for a while. Then . . ." She pushed windblown hair from her eyes. "Something happened, I don't know what, and it all changed. There's this man you haven't seen yet, I don't think. Jax. He's Holix's best friend. We all thought he was in charge, because he always brought us our instructions."

"From your father?" Iolaus asked.

"I guess so. Who else? Anyway, Rotus decided Jax didn't know what he was doing. Whenever Jax wasn't around, Rotus made up his own plans. I didn't like them. He wanted people hurt."

Iolaus didn't get it. "So why didn't you say anything?"

"Rotus said he'd cut my throat."

Iolaus' eyes widened. "He . . . what? Your throat? He did?" His eyes narrowed, his face hardened, but he only grunted, nothing more.

Hercules shook his head in disbelief. Themon was the damnedest place he had ever visited. It had a peacetime tyrant who wasn't all that bad, a band of rebels that kept changing its mind about how serious it was about its revolution, a festival that once in a while sacrificed its queen, and a street nearly a half mile long with no buildings on it.

It was . . .

His mouth opened.

It was . . .

"Herc?"

Again he stared at the city, and the sea.

"What's the matter with him?" Venitia whispered.

"He's thinking."

"Oh."

"No, not just 'oh.' *Uh*-oh."

"Uh-oh?" she asked.

Iolaus nodded. "Uh-oh as in trouble," Iolaus explained.

"But there already *is* trouble."

Iolaus shook his head. "When he gets like this, you have no idea what trouble really means."

Ignoring their commentary, Hercules lowered himself to his hands and knees and leaned over the edge of the cliff. With the tide out, the sand below was nearly dry; clumps of drying kelp clung to the shadows of the jagged boulders; the sea-sharpened edges of brown-black rock poked out of the cliff's face. He couldn't see the base of the cliff because there was a slight overhang, and he chided himself for not inspecting the area last night.

Iolaus knelt beside him, questioning him with a look.

Hercules rocked back on his heels. "A shrine," he explained. "There has to be a shrine around here somewhere. To help draw Hera here.'' He gestured. ''Everything is too open, Iolaus, or we would have seen it by now.''

''Shrine?'' Venitia said, puzzled.

''To Hera,'' Iolaus told her.

The woman shook her head. ''Not here. Demeter, Poseidon, a couple of others, but not Hera. Not here.''

For no reason other than instinct, Hercules knew she was wrong. However, a check of the sun told him the festival would start soon, and he and Iolaus would be expected in the plaza.

Too much to do and not much time left to do it.

His expression brooking no arguments, he told Iolaus to search the area from here to the fishing center for something that might be used as a shrine; Venitia he sent off to the rebels, with instructions to find out what, exactly, Rotus planned to do during the festivities.

He himself hurried back to the Red Boar, surprised that he didn't get lost more than once. Maybe twice, but he couldn't really tell, because he was lost.

When he reached the inn, he hurried straight to his room, pushed open the door, and froze.

Holix still lay on the bed.

A woman sat beside him, a gleaming knife in her hand.

16

"Hercules, no!" Holix cried hoarsely when Hercules slammed the door behind him and took a long stride toward the bed. "It's all right, really, it's all right!"

Fortunately, Hercules had already figured that out by the way the woman had scrambled onto the bed and done her best to push herself into the wall.

The knife fell harmlessly to the floor.

"Hercules?" the woman breathed.

Holix nodded. "Yes. He saved my life."

She was, Hercules thought, extraordinarily beautiful, with rich red hair that must be the envy of many a goddess. Keeping his palms up to show he wasn't going to harm her, he pulled the chair closer to the bed and sank into it. Smiled. Tilted his head to tell the young man he was ready to listen.

With much theatrical moaning and groaning and wincing and hissing, Holix pushed himself to a sitting position, his back against the wall behind the low headboard. A clean cloth had been wrapped around his head, his face washed of grime and blood, and a fresh, deep-green tunic replaced his tattered old one.

"This is Cire," he said, trying to sound casual without revealing how smitten he was. Which, of course, is exactly what he revealed.

"I ran away," she said in a fearful whisper, explaining that the streets had been filled with the talk of the battle that had occurred that day at the stable. When she'd raced there to find Holix, a number of people told her he'd been carried away by a giant. "You, I guess."

Hercules didn't know how to respond. Once again he was uncomfortable at the awe his name inspired. He gestured weakly, smiled, then listened with increasing anger as Cire recounted what she had overheard in the house where she and her twin worked. Her eyes reddened, her lips trembled, and by the time she finished, a tear had begun to trickle down her cheek.

Hercules sat back and crossed his legs, staring thoughtfully at the window. "For one thing," he said, "you aren't going to die."

"See?" Holix said. "I told you."

"And I'm pretty sure I know what's really going on."

Holix grinned. "See? I told you."

Hercules hushed him with a glance. "For another, though, Cire, you'll have to go back."

"See?" Holix said. "I . . . what?"

"What?" Cire echoed. "Holix, where's the knife?"

Hercules hushed them again, this time with a scowl that sent them into each other's arms. Gingerly, however, since Holix's ribs had not miraculously healed.

Hercules' gaze returned to the window. "What happened to Bea?"

"She left when I arrived," Cire answered flatly, her head resting possessively against Holix's shoulder. "He didn't need her anymore."

Hercules grunted.

She raised her head. "And what do you mean, I have to go back? Do you know what's supposed to happen if I do?"

"Yes."

"I'm supposed to die!"

"I know."

Cire struggled to sit upright, bracing a palm against Holix's chest. The stable hand promptly opened his mouth in a silent scream. "So I'm not going."

"Yes, you are," Hercules told her.

"Holix, where's the damn knife?"

Holix gasped; he couldn't do anything else.

"You have to go back," Hercules told her calmly. "It's the only way I can save you. And us."

"Never mind," she grumbled as she started to crawl across Holix's legs. "I'll get it myself."

Hercules didn't bother to look this time—he snared her arm and eased her back onto the bed, squeezed once in a silent order to stay put, and propped his feet on the lumpy mattress, crossing them at the ankles.

With any kind of luck, he would appear more confident than he felt.

Which was, right now, hardly confident at all.

"Look," he said, "I know it won't help much, but this whole thing isn't really about you."

Cire snorted. "Yeah, right."

Hercules explained. "I'm the one who's supposed to die. Not you."

Holix gasped, and blinked away a few tears of lingering agony.

"Okay with me," Cire said, then started when Holix gasped again and she realized she had been leaning her elbow against his bruised sternum. What followed was a few minutes of tearful apologies, some well-placed kisses, and Holix's valiant attempts to bear it all without screaming.

I am blessed by the gods, Hercules thought wearily . . . and when I find which ones did it, I'm going to thump them.

"Tonight," he said when Holix had been soothed and Cire was at last listening, "I'm going to find out exactly how involved Titus is in this. Not the rebels. That's a different matter, and I'm not sure how it fits. Or even if it does. I need to know what Titus knows, and that I can't do until later. And until I do find out, we have to carry on as if we don't know anything. In other words, look and act normal."

Cire opened her mouth to remind him that acting normal, for her, in this situation, would get her fairly dead, but changed her mind and shook her head instead.

He smiled at her confusion. "You don't know me, Cire, but you'll have to trust me. I don't intend to let you die, and I certainly don't intend to die myself." He tapped a finger against his temple. "I only have a vague idea of what's really happening around here. But if I'm right—"

He cut himself off.

They didn't need to hear it.

They didn't need to know that if he was indeed right, saving Cire from the Klothon wouldn't do her any good.

She would die anyway.

Iolaus danced nimbly away from the hiss and foam of an approaching wave, and cursed the day he had accepted the stupid invitation to judge this stupid queen thing at this stupid festival thing.

It was supposed to be fun.

What it was, was misery.

He was soaked from the ocean's spray. His left shin was banged up from an encounter with an outcropping he hadn't seen because he had been too intent on not getting slammed by a wave. He absolutely did not like the rocks looming darkly over him, or the way those gulls stared at him with their flat black eyes. And as long as he was at it, he didn't understand why Hercules had sent Venitia off on an errand he knew full well was going to net her nothing.

He had made his way along the beach from the fishing wharf and had found zilch. As he had expected. His first pass along the cliff's base had been a failure as well, but he was sure a shrine was here somewhere. It had to be. Unless it was invisible.

And why not? he thought. An invisible shrine would make about as much sense as anything else these days.

On the other hand, this search at least gave him some respite from Venitia. Not that she was a terrible person or anything, and not that he wouldn't mind celebrating with her sometime during his stay, and not that he wasn't flattered by her attention.

But the sheer intensity of that attention was, to say the least, unnerving. It was as if he had walked into Themon with a target on his forehead, and she was determined to hit the bull's-eye. One way or another.

"Boy," he muttered, and stared at the rock wall, sidestepping as he did.

It all looked alike to him—brown rock glistening with spray, barnacles, streaks of droppings from the gulls, piles of kelp where the tide had left them . . . if this was somehow Hera's local shrine, no wonder she was in a lousy mood all the time.

A wave tickled his boot soles.

A gull screamed at him.

A larger wave slapped his ankles, and he whirled angrily, ready to draw his sword, until he realized the absurdity of threatening the sea with his weapon.

Getting to me, he decided; this whole place is getting to me.

By the time he reached the first, and tallest, of the dragon's-teeth rocks, he was ready to give up. His shadow had already shifted from his right to his left, and if he was going to make it back to the inn before the evening ceremonies, he'd better leave soon.

Another gull screamed just as a wave shattered against an outer rock.

The sound of wings.

He looked up just in time to see a large black-faced gull sweep down at his head. He ducked, instinctively swinging one arm up for protection, and grimaced when he felt the bird slam against the blade.

"Great," he muttered as he stood. "Great."

The bird was at the cliff's base, a single feather on an upraised wing fluttering in the breeze.

"Great."

He walked over and glared down at it. "Stupid bird. Haven't you ever seen a sword before?"

At that moment he heard yet another scream, and ducked again, yelling at the gulls to leave him alone.

They refused to comply.

At least a half dozen swooped from shallow ledges on the rocks and dove at his skull and eyes. Screaming. Batting at his face and shoulders with their wings. One dropping under a halfhearted swing of the sword to nip his neck and draw blood.

For a few moments he was confused. There were too many feathers, too many wings, too many sharp beaks for him to know which way to turn. He had been using the sword without much enthusiasm, not wanting to have to kill another bird. The gulls, however, weren't as timid, and when a talon raked across his brow, Iolaus lost his temper.

With a shout, he stood to his full height and aimed his sword at the cloud of gulls swarming around him.

It did no good.

For every bird he drove away or brought to the ground, three more joined the fray, and there was nothing for it but to run.

So he ran.

And he hadn't gone four strides before he realized he was running straight at the cliff, the gulls battering him, deafening him, nearly blinding him.

It was too late to veer away, and he braced himself for the collision.

Except there wasn't one.

One minute he was about to dash himself against solid rock, and the next he found himself in a tunnel whose entrance had been hidden by the convoluted configuration of the cliff face.

The gulls didn't follow.

It took him a few seconds to understand what had happened, a few seconds more before he was able to walk without his legs wobbling.

He didn't go very far.

Light from outside reached only a few yards into the tunnel, and he wasn't about to poke around in the dark, risking a broken limb, or worse, just to find proof of what he already knew: that somewhere at the tunnel's end was Hera's shrine. He was no coward, had been in many battles and had faced many creatures that weren't remotely human, but Hera . . . she was not to be tempted.

This, he thought, was a job for Hercules.

All he had to do was survive the onslaught of birds so he could tell him.

Cire still wanted to know where the knife was.

It was under Hercules' rump, but he wasn't about to tell her that. What he did tell her, and Holix, was the nugget of a plan he believed might work. But only if they did exactly what they were told.

When he explained what they were to do, fleshing out the idea as he spoke, Cire told him flatly that it couldn't work, wouldn't work, and they were all going to die.

Holix told him he didn't think he'd be able to walk, much less do what he was supposed to do.

Hercules told them both that walking would be the least of their problems if they didn't stop complaining and pay attention.

At this point Cire decided that she didn't need the knife, her nails were long enough.

Hercules ignored her. "You'll never have to work in a stable again," he said to Holix. And when he saw the look on the young man's face, he wished he'd thought of that sooner.

"Really?"

"Of course," Cire said sourly. "Because you'll be dead. I'll be dead. We'll be—"

"The question is," Hercules interrupted, "can you do it?"

Holix looked at Cire, and hushed her abruptly, his hand reaching out and brushing her cheek. "For her, I can do anything."

Without warning Cire began to weep.

Slowly Hercules lowered his feet to the floor and stood. There was nothing more to say. What he needed was to leave these two alone for a few minutes while he waited for Iolaus; what he needed was a sign that a fair amount of luck was heading his way; and finally, what he needed most was a new head, because this was one of the dumbest, riskiest, most dangerous things he had ever done.

Even Iolaus, with his unbounded enthusiasm and

general lack of foresight, couldn't possibly have come up with something as stupid as this.

The door slammed open, interrupting Hercules' self-deprecating reverie.

Cire uttered a short scream, Holix a longer gasping one.

"Herc," Iolaus exclaimed, "you're not going to believe it."

Hercules stared at him. "You're soaked."

Iolaus blinked several drops of water out of his eyes. "Of course I'm soaked. I've been fighting killer seagulls and huge tides just to get back here."

"Killer *what*?"

Glowering, Iolaus clamped his hands onto his hips. "Do you want to know what I found or what?"

It was a toss-up, fifty-fifty, but the expression on Iolaus' face made the choice for him. "A shrine?"

Iolaus pointed at the window. "You'd better have a look. Then I hope you have a plan, because, boy, we're going to need one."

17

The boulevard was jammed with participants and spectators for the festival's first parade.

Litters borne on the shoulders of rippling-muscled slaves carried the jewel-bedecked elite, who tossed dinars and trinkets into the crowd lining the broad street; chariots with plumed, high-stepping horses rattled slowly over the paving stones; on a long narrow platform held aloft by a score of capped acolytes in gold-and-emerald tunics rode a shrine to Demeter, surrounded with representations of the harvest yet to come; a band of trumpeters and drummers marched behind a squad of Themonian guards; another shrine glided past, this one dedicated to the daily harvest of fish provided by Poseidon.

The music, the cheering, the applause, the cries of hopeful prayers as each shrine passed—all of it blithely continued despite the darkening sky above.

Hercules and Iolaus hurried toward the plaza as best they could, forcing themselves to smile as men grabbed their hands to shake them, and ladies flung their arms around their necks to plant kisses.

At another time, Iolaus would have been in his element. Now he could only frown his skepticism.

"You're kidding. That's the plan?" he asked Hercules.

"It's better than 'run.'"

"In case you've forgotten, 'run' worked."

"So will this."

"Are you sure?"

"Pretty sure."

"What if you're wrong?"

"I'm not wrong, Iolaus."

"Because of a dream."

"Yes. Because of a dream."

The frown deepened, then vanished abruptly as Iolaus grinned. "Well, why not? I can remember times when we had a lot less to go on."

The side streets had become rivers of people, all taking favorite shortcuts, all trying to get to the plaza in time, all hoping they would find a good place to watch the festival begin. A few fights broke out, a few purses were snatched, but no one seemed to care. Part of it was the atmosphere, but most of it was because there were so many people that the thieves seldom got very far before they were caught, thumped, and left behind to try again.

At the garden entrance to a small but imposing estate not far from the plaza, there was relative peace. The cacophony of the festival hadn't yet reached this section of the city; right now it was only a muffled din.

"Holix, are you sure this is the right thing to do?" Cire asked.

"What choice do we have?"

"We could run. Now."

"No. We have to trust Hercules."

"I'm frightened."

"Don't worry. I'll be there."

"Oh sure."

"Cire, don't do this. We have to give Hercules a chance."

"I know, but it's you I'm worried about."

"Why?"

"What if you fall off?"

"I won't."

"What if you hurt yourself again?"

"Again? How can I be more hurt than I already am?"

"You could be dead."

"Yes, well . . ."

She threw her arms around him, kissed him so soundly he barely felt the pain in his ribs, his head, his right arm, his right leg, and along his back. When she broke the embrace, he grinned at her stupidly.

She laughed. "You look silly."

"Maybe, but I'm screaming inside."

In the fishing quarter, men and women rushed to secure their boats. The small fleet had quit early, and the people were anxious to join the celebration. They weren't concerned about their profits. On festival day the council made up the shortfall out of the public treasury, aided by a few private donations.

What the council didn't know this year, however, is the relief the fishermen felt.

Maybe the city fathers couldn't count, but these people could.

This was the seventh year, and no one wanted to be on the water.

In the grove outside the rebel cave, Rotus sneered at the crumpled body lying at his feet.

"That," he said to the others, "is what happens to all traitors."

One of the rebels shuddered. "Hercules is going to be ticked when he finds out."

"I can handle Hercules. Don't worry about that."

None of the rebels responded, although a couple of them turned quickly to their horses, anxious to be away.

"Remember the signal," Rotus told them once they were all mounted.

"What signal?"

"The one I told you."

The rebels shook their heads. "You didn't tell us any signal," one dared say.

Rotus rolled his eyes. "I did. You weren't listening."

"I was too listening. Your trouble is, you mumble all the time."

"I do not mumble. I enunciate."

"What's that?"

"I speak clearly."

"Well, sure you do, Rotus. When you're not mumbling."

Rotus glared, sighed, repeated the signal, and led them at a gallop away from the cave.

Less than a minute later a raven settled on Jax's body, cocked its head, and tried to decide where it would begin its dinner.

The household was in an uproar about Cire's behavior. The master threatened to take the girl's head and exhibit it on a stake at the garden gate; the mistress, on the other hand, didn't want to wait for the head to come off.

Only when Sana reminded them that the council was waiting did they swallow their anger and order Cire dressed.

When they were alone, the twins looked at each other tearfully.

"I'm so happy," Sana said, wiping her eyes delicately with one finger. She wore a rippling, floor-length shift, elegantly embroidered with silver thread, and a heavy necklace. Her red hair was pulled back behind her ears and braided, the braid twined with rainbow ribbons. On her head she wore a simple laurel wreath.

"I am, too," Cire told her, forcing herself to sound cheerful.

"Do you think they'll pick me?"

"You're the prettier of the two of us."

"But how will they know that?"

"Sana!"

"I'm joking, Sister, just joking. Now hold still, I have to brush your hair. What a mess!"

"It's windy."

"So . . . are you going to tell me where you were?"

"No. I can't."

"A man, right?"

"I can't."

"That means you won't."

"Whatever."

"Stop fidgeting, Sister. How can I make you pretty if you keep fidgeting all the time?"

"Gods, Sana, just give me my sandals and the damn wreath and let's get out of here."

"My, my, we're testy tonight, aren't we?"

"Sorry. It's the . . . excitement."

"I know, I know. I can't wait, can you? Of course you can't. I can see it in your eyes."

Cire nodded, closed her eyes in a brief prayer for miracles and Holix not falling off and ruining the plan, and headed for the exit.

"Cire?"

"What now?"

"Your sandals are on backward."

Venitia had no one to talk to.

She hadn't been able to locate any of the rebels, her mother had already left, her father was with the council in its chambers, Iolaus was with Hercules, she didn't trust the servants, and Bea was with whomever she was with, probably a man, probably one of the guard officers.

She didn't bother with Zarel. That woman was

probably with Rotus and the others, sharpening her knife, her nails, and her tongue.

Thus abandoned, she dressed alone.

In a way that was good, because the outfit she chose exposed more of her than her father would like. Considerably more. Although, if the truth be told and he had his way, she'd be wearing a sack all the time anyway, only her eyes and feet showing.

Iolaus, on the other hand, had better come up with the right reaction when he saw her, or she'd be forced to do something drastic. Like get him alone, wear him down, and carry him home over her shoulder. Figuratively speaking, of course. Mother would never approve, otherwise.

She sighed.

She shivered.

The festival was supposed to be fun. Parties, food, wine, messing around, getting in trouble with Father and getting out of trouble with Father . . . in short, fun.

But this time everything had gone wrong. The rebellion wasn't fun anymore, and with Iolaus muttering all the time about monsters and vengeful goddesses, she feared people were going to get hurt, or worse.

Still, she thought, with Hercules around, how bad could it get?

"Herc, what's the worst thing that can happen if we don't pull this off?"

"I don't want to think about it."

"That bad?"

"That bad."

Iolaus followed him around the plaza's perimeter, heading for the steps. "I want to get something straight, okay? If this doesn't work, the festival will be ruined, a monster will show up and people will die, Demeter and Poseidon will be pissed because their festival was ruined, Hera will win, and if I survive, I'll have about half a dozen gods chasing after me for the rest of my life."

Hercules thought about it a while before saying, "Yep, that about covers it."

Iolaus stopped.

Hercules stopped, turned, and said with a soft smile, "Would you have it any other way?"

Iolaus laughed. "No, I guess not."

They shook hands then, and embraced briefly.

Then they stepped out of the crowd into the plaza, and Iolaus whispered, "Oh, my."

18

The plaza had been transformed into a miniature amphitheater. Small columns, holding large pans of oil that would be lit when the sun dropped below the rooftops, had been placed beside the marble colonnade. The stands were now over a dozen rows high and swept away from each side of the municipal building's steps in a gentle arc that remained open where the boulevard began.

They were jammed, the wealthy sitting nearest the steps, the ordinary citizens taking all the other places. In addition, people sat on the ground behind long red ropes attached to gleaming brass posts; and nearby rooftops were crowded with those who hadn't been able to squeeze into the plaza.

On the chamber porch, beneath the blossom-covered peaked roof, were three tables covered with white cloth, facing the plaza, each with a row of ornately carved high-back chairs behind them. On the left sat dignitaries and their wives from the surrounding villages and inland farm towns, puffed with importance and already flushed with wine. The center table held the council. The right was empty, reserved for the women who would be competing for the title of festival queen.

Hercules and Iolaus sat at the center table.

Iolaus gaped at the platters of food and jugs of wine spread before him. "Gods, what am I supposed to do now?"

Hercules laughed. "Eat, what else?"

"What, with all those people staring at me?"

And they were—hundreds of them, in the stands and on the ground, their own food and wineskins in their laps, their attention torn between picking out the famous and not so famous at the head tables, and the entertainment that played continuously in the plaza's center. Musicians, dance troupes, jugglers, trick riders, mock swordplay, gymnasts: each act had its brief turn before being replaced by another. There was no ringmaster and no introductions, just one act after another.

Hercules barely noticed.

Ever since his and Iolaus' arrival, they had been swamped with men and women proclaiming their favorites for the summer queen, not bothering to listen when he told them he didn't even know who the candidates were. Finally one of the councilman had taken over, insisting they wear garlands of flowers as a sign of their standing, then dragging them from chair to chair, introducing them to everyone as if bringing them here was his own idea.

Shortly after they finally escaped to their own seats, Venitia grabbed the chair to Iolaus' right. To Hercules' left was a suspiciously large gap between himself and Jocasta Perical. His attempts to speak to either Titus or his wife had thus far failed miserably. The man kept himself busy with orders to the servants and guards, so much so that Hercules began to wonder if the council leader was avoiding him. Jocasta proved just as elusive; she seemed to make sure she was seldom seated, fussing constantly over the comfort of her other guests.

Iolaus wasn't much help either.

He didn't know how Venitia managed it, but she wore a clinging and somewhat translucent dress that evidently came with a magic red shawl, one that remained demurely draped over her shoulders and chest whenever her father was around, and somehow vanished whenever he wasn't.

Iolaus had obviously noticed the dress—and all that it revealed—and tried so terribly hard not to that Hercules couldn't help but laugh.

Incorrigible; the man was incorrigible.

And apparently doomed to break his neck, when his attention became torn between Venitia's blatant efforts at flirtation and the afternoon's final performance—an all-female dance ensemble from the Isle of Minnsci. They were lovely and lithe, and forever stumbling and losing the veils that barely concealed their barely concealing costumes.

The crowd loved it.

Iolaus loved it.

Venitia hated it and damn near plunked herself in Iolaus' lap to get him to pay attention to her, not them.

Hercules admitted that he himself was not entirely

immune to the ladies' charms as they danced out of the plaza, but at the moment he was more concerned with what he saw above Themon.

He nudged Iolaus with an elbow. "Look."

"I am," Iolaus said without turning around.

Venitia giggled.

"Not that," Hercules said, rapping his friend's skull with a knuckle. He pointed to the east. "That."

Although the sun still shone brightly over the city, the sky over the distant sea was filled with clouds. Black clouds laced with sickly gray, shifting constantly, expanding, every once in a while flaring with hidden lightning.

Iolaus watched the clouds for several seconds. "They aren't moving."

"Not yet."

"How much time?"

Hercules shook his head.

This was the tricky part of his half-formed plan. Actually, there were lots of tricky parts to the plan, most of them unavoidable because he had no real idea exactly how Hera would set things in motion. He had been tempted to try to contact Poseidon again, but there'd been no time. All he had left was his instinct, and a finely tuned sense of self-preservation.

Movement to his left made him turn, just in time to see a messenger whisper something in Jocasta's ear. She stiffened, and the eye Hercules could see instantly brimmed with tears. She nodded at another word, dismissed the boy with a gesture, and pushed away from the table. As Titus strode by she took his arm, said something, and pulled him away.

Now, Hercules thought; it has to be now.

The plaza fell silent.

Although conversations were still whispered in the stands, and among those who sat around the perimeter, there was no laughter, no cheers, only a communal sense of delighted anticipation.

Hercules waited until Titus and his wife approached the tall brass doors before leaving his seat. He crossed the porch quickly, before anyone could intercept him, and reached them just as Jocasta said, ''They found him by the cave. The others were gone.''

Seeing Hercules approach, Titus shook his head slightly in warning and beamed at his guest. ''Hercules! I certainly hope you're enjoying our little celebration.'' He took him by the elbow. ''Why don't we just return to our seats? The finale is about to—''

Hercules didn't budge. ''What did Hera promise you?'' he said, keeping his voice low.

Titus blinked. ''What did . . . what are you talking about?''

Hercules held out his left arm to prevent Jocasta from leaving, the smile at his lips completely without mirth. ''You know what I mean.''

He waited, hoping his expression explained to them both that he was giving them only this one chance.

Jocasta touched her husband's arm. ''Titus.'' It was a plea.

The councillor drew himself up, one hand at his chest.

"Titus," she said again.

Hercules glanced at the tables; no one, yet, was watching. "Whatever it was, Titus, she lied."

Suddenly Titus was an old man. His shoulders sagged, his chest deflated, and there was a look of defeat in his eyes that made Hercules wince.

"This," the politician said hoarsely, taking in the guests, the plaza, and the city with a slow sweeping gesture. "All I had to do was one small favor, and I could keep all this until I was ready to retire." He gave Hercules and Jocasta a one-sided, bitter smile. "And something else."

Hercules watched him closely.

Titus glanced at the sky, at the clouds gathering on the horizon. "If I didn't do it," he said softly, "she swore to murder my family. My daughter. My wife. Take them both, and then destroy the city. My . . . curse." The bitter smile became a brief bitter laugh. "I suppose it was too much to hope for, that she would keep her word."

"From Hera, yes," Hercules said bluntly. He put a hand to his mouth, thinking fast. "She kept you in power all this time?"

"No," Jocasta answered angrily. "He's a good man, Hercules. A little wrongheaded sometimes, a little stubborn." She leaned into her husband, forcing him to put an arm around her waist. "A little behind the times every once in a while, that's all." Her tone hardened. "But he was good for Themon. Good. You can see that. All you have to do is look."

"And the rebels?" Hercules wanted to know.

This time it was her smile that was one-sided. "My idea. He didn't even know about it until this year. It was the only way we could get him to keep up sometimes."

Hercules looked at them both with near admiration. "You," he said to Titus, "couldn't stop. And you, you want him to step down."

Now her smile was genuine. "I've been packing all day. We were going to leave tomorrow night."

"We have a small place," Titus said. "Near the foothills. Quiet. No seagulls. Nobody cares who I am out there." His shoulders rose and fell in a sigh. "So what happens now?" He didn't wait for an answer. He looked out over the plaza, at the people shifting in the stands. "Hera lied."

"That's one of her good points," Hercules said. "She's after me, Titus. That's why she had you invite Iolaus. Because she knew I'd come along. And to get to me, she'll do anything. Including destroying this city and everyone in it." He paused, shook his head. "And when she was done, she would have come after you anyway."

Flustered, Titus took a step toward the tables, stopped, and shook his head. "But we can't just stop the festival. I mean, all those people . . . the gods will be . . ." He clasped his hands and brought them to his lips. His eyes narrowed. "You knew all this, and still you're here? Doing nothing?"

"Titus," Jocasta warned softly.

"No. This man knows, and he's not doing a damn thing but eating our food and drinking our wine and

169

... and ..." He sputtered into silence when he couldn't think of anything else to say.

"There's a plan," Hercules said, more to Jocasta than to her husband.

"How can we help?" she asked.

"All you have to do is not get in the way."

"In the way of what?" Titus demanded, his voice breaking.

"Of the plan."

"What plan?"

"My plan."

"Which is?"

Hercules shook his head. "I can't tell you."

"He can't tell us," the man said to Jocasta.

"That's part of the plan," Hercules said, beginning to feel a little trapped. Maybe a little tap to the man's jaw would do it. Not too hard. Just enough to put him to sleep for a couple of hours.

Titus stuck his chin out.

Hercules restrained himself.

"What. Plan."

Hercules looked down at his right hand, saw the fist, and ordered it to open. When he was sure it wouldn't do anything on its own, he noticed that the guests and the people in the stands were growing restless. Quickly, then, he took Jocasta's arm and led her toward the center table, Titus stamping along behind.

"I told you," she said. "Stubborn sometimes."

"You must really love him," he said, only half seriously.

"Oh, I do. It isn't always easy, but I do."

At the table he waited until she was seated. When

Titus, grumbling and swearing under his breath, joined them, Hercules instructed them to do what they always did, but not to be surprised by what happened next.

"What's going to happen next?" Titus asked in a whisper loud enough to be heard all the way to Athens.

"The plan," Hercules reminded him.

"What plan?"

The plan, Hercules told him with an exasperated look, *that starts with you leaving Themon feet-first if you don't stop asking me what plan.*

Titus closed his mouth so tightly his lips disappeared.

Hercules nodded sharply—*good man, you get to live.*

After taking his own seat and automatically picking up a piece of bread from the platter in front of him, he watched as Iolaus concentrated on Venitia, as Jocasta tried to soothe and reassure her husband, as the people in the plaza began to stamp their feet and clap their hands with impatience, as the storm continued to build darkly on the horizon.

He pushed a nervous hand back through his hair.

He felt the slow breeze that coasted up the boulevard into the makeshift amphitheater, catching the scent of salt and rain.

I'm right, he told himself; I know I'm right.

But when it happened, he knew it would happen fast.

He only hoped he was ready.

19

Titus Perical rose from his seat and stepped around to the front of the center table. At the top of the steps he lifted his arms, and after an intricate flourish of trumpets, the crowd rose to its feet and cheered.

Hercules glanced at Jocasta, and saw the pride on her face, and a deep melancholy that made him look away.

A look at Iolaus, however, caused him to worry. His friend's cheeks were flushed, and the way he leaned close to Venitia, Hercules was afraid the man had drunk too much wine.

The trumpets sounded again.

Iolaus leaned close. "This is it?"

Hercules nodded.

"It's about time." Iolaus lowered his voice. "This woman is driving me crazy."

"I thought you enjoyed it," Hercules said dryly.

Iolaus made a face at him—*of course I enjoyed it, you dope*—lifted his goblet, and brought it to his lips. His throat moved, his eyes half closed, but when the

172

goblet was set back on the table, the level hadn't dropped more than a sip.

When Hercules stared, Iolaus winked.

At that moment the crowd settled into an excited murmuring as, far to the left, a procession made its way down the eight broad steps. It was, he realized, the shrine he had seen earlier in the parade. It was carried to the center of the plaza and set carefully on the ground.

A single trumpet blew a single sweet note.

Hercules swallowed hard.

The crowd took to its feet again when Titus gestured grandly, and the acolytes who had carried the shrine into the plaza returned in two rows. Between the rows were five women, all dressed alike, heads bowed, feet bare.

Venitia squeaked with delight. "Boy, I wish I were one of them."

Iolaus gave her an *are you nuts?* look.

She shrugged. "Okay, I don't. Well, I do, but not really. I mean—" She shut up and grabbed a goblet.

It was easy to spot Cire and her twin because of their red hair, walking one behind the other in the center of the line. At this distance it was impossible to tell which was which. Until one of them stumbled slightly, and Hercules knew that was Cire.

He leaned toward Jocasta. "Do they stay down there?"

She shook her head, but said nothing.

The line of women left the priestly acolytes and made a circuit around the shrine before moving to the foot of the steps. In a speech Hercules figured he delivered every year, Titus greeted them as though they were true queens, praising their beauty and impressing upon them the importance and solemnity of their office, however temporary it might be.

The crowd had fallen silent.

The speech went on, and each time Titus mentioned either Demeter or Poseidon, he made a sharp gesture with his left hand, bringing the women up one step at a time.

Hercules knew that when they reached the top, it would be time for him and Iolaus to act. What he didn't know was how Titus would get them to single out Cire.

Iolaus squirmed impatiently.

"How long does this go on?" Hercules asked Jocasta.

She sighed with a faint smile. "Forever, Hercules, forever. He's a politician, remember?"

She was right.

Even when the contestants reached the top step, Titus continued to speak. He stood in front of them now, his voice carrying easily as he recounted each woman's history and described what she had promised to bring to this solemn office should she be chosen by the heroes who had traveled all this way just for this moment.

Iolaus whispered, "Am I still awake?"

Hercules coughed into a fist to keep from laughing.

The crowd, however, didn't seem to mind. Cheers were offered at regular intervals; feet stomped as if on cue; ribbons and scarves were waved like flags; even those jammed into the gap where the plaza met the boulevard, and those on the nearby rooftops, found ways of signaling their approval.

Titus spoke on. Eloquently. Movingly. Interminably. Switching to describe the city's devotion to the gods who were the patrons of this occasion. Seamlessly weaving praise for them into praise for Hercules and Iolaus.

Iolaus kept squirming. "You'd think we were gods, too," he muttered, looked at Hercules, and added, "Well, some of us, anyway. Partly, at least. Sort of."

Hercules hushed him with a look, at the same time reminding him to keep his eye on the plaza. For anything that seemed unusual.

Then he heard a curious noise behind him, checked over his shoulder, and saw one of the huge brass-paneled doors begin to swing open. He frowned. With all the councillors out here, Titus blathering out there, and the guards all in place by each pillar and ranged along each step, who would be back by the doors?

His eyes widened.

"Iolaus," he snapped, and with a polite smile for no one in particular, he eased his chair back and stood.

"What, already?" Iolaus said. He frowned at the plaza. "But I don't see—"

Hercules moved swiftly to the back of the porch, just to the left of the partially open door. Although the crowd was still noisy, he heard the distinct sound of metal softly striking metal. "Company," he whispered when Iolaus joined him, and pointed at the widening gaps between the doors.

Iolaus nodded, and rubbed his hands together.

175

Hercules almost grinned. Beautiful women and a fight—Iolaus was in his element, no question about it.

However, they didn't dare let the intruders loose on the porch. Chaos would result, and too many bodies.

He took a deep breath and placed his palms against the door.

Iolaus tilted his head back to measure the door's height and width, and mouthed, *It looks damn big and heavy, Herc.*

No kidding, thought Hercules, who took another breath, braced himself, and pushed lightly so he'd know just how heavy it was.

Then, without hesitation, he shoved it.

Hard.

There were yelps of surprise and pain as the door swung shut, more cries when Hercules yanked it open again and he and Iolaus slid quickly into the gap.

The first thing Hercules saw was a half-dozen ropes dangling from the gap in the broad corridor's ceiling.

The second thing he saw was three men sprawled on the floor, fumbling for their weapons.

The third thing was Rotus, halfway down one of the ropes, gaping in astonishment as Iolaus, wasting no time, waded into the rebels with the flat of his sword, and a fist.

There was no time for anything fancy. One rebel sagged when the fist caught his chin. Another dropped when the sword smacked him across the cheek, laying open skin even as the rebel collapsed. A third Iolaus clipped under the jaw with the heel of his boot.

176

Trusting his friend to watch his back, Hercules ran for the rope Rotus was now desperately trying to climb back up. When he reached it, he grabbed it and yanked as he said, "Nice of you to hang around."

The rope snapped as if it were straw.

Rotus fell with a shriek.

Hercules caught him, grinned, dropped him, picked him up under the shoulders, and slammed him into the wall.

Rotus sighed and toppled forward.

Hercules let him fall.

And grunted when a fist clubbed him on the spine. He turned to face a man . . . he blinked. It was a woman, with long black hair and raging green eyes, who hadn't expected him to turn. Instantly he reached out and clamped a hand on her head. She swung again, but her reach wasn't long enough, and Hercules forced her to his knees, leaned over, and said, "If you want to live, friend, stay where you are and don't move."

When he released her, Zarel tensed as if to charge.

"I don't care if you're a woman or not," Hercules warned with a growl, and showed her his fist. "I've no time to be polite. Don't. Move."

The rage in her eyes slipped quickly into outright fear, and she obeyed, frozen as a statue, lower lip quivering violently.

Meanwhile, Iolaus had been backed against the doors by the two remaining rebels, one wildly swinging a sword at his midsection while the other danced from side to side, looking for a way to slip his own weapon under Iolaus' guard.

"Hey!" Iolaus called when he saw Hercules watching.

Hercules waved.

Iolaus frowned, ducked, lashed out with a foot, ducked, sidestepped, and yelled, "Hey!"

Hercules walked over to Rotus and planted a boot on his back when he noticed the man beginning to stir.

"Hey, dammit!"

Hercules pointed at the fallen leader. "I've got my hands full."

Iolaus rolled his eyes in disgust, dodged a swing, ducked another, hesitated just long enough for one of the men to lunge, then sidestepped again.

The rebel sword stabbed into the door, snapping in half and momentarily stunning its wielder. That was just long enough for Iolaus to put a foot into the rebel's chest and tumble him backward, allowing him, Iolaus, to turn his full attention to the second man.

Who, as it turned out, wasn't too happy about such attention.

He backed away.

Iolaus' lips parted in a shark's smile, and he stepped forward.

The rebel spun around to run, saw Hercules, spun back to defend himself, and dropped instantly when Iolaus clubbed him right in the center of his forehead.

For a second the only noise was the sound of harsh breathing. And a couple of faint moans. And the muffled roar of the crowd.

Iolaus stomped over to Hercules, not bothering to step over the bodies he encountered.

"You could have helped."

Hercules pointed downward. "I didn't want him to get away."

"You're standing on him, for crying out loud! How's he going to get away?"

"If I helped you, I wouldn't be standing on him."

Frustrated, Iolaus slapped his thigh. "I have to do everything around here, don't I? Everything." He checked himself over and groaned. "Look at me! I'm all sweaty! How am I going to judge those women when I'm all sweaty!"

"Venitia will love it."

Iolaus glared. "Not funny, Herc. Not funny."

Hercules thought it was, but Iolaus obviously wasn't in the mood for pleasantries. So he suggested they summon the guards to take care of the prisoners so they themselves could get back outside and prepare for the next step.

Iolaus agreed, then stepped back and looked askance at his friend. "But you're not going to tell me this was part of the plan."

Hercules shrugged.

Iolaus pointed a trembling finger at him. "You . . ." He pointed at Rotus. "He . . ." He pointed at the doors just as the left one swung open. "They . . ." He slumped a little. "Not part of the plan."

"We knew they were coming."

"We *thought* they *might* come."

"They did, right?"

Iolaus' face reddened. "But it wasn't part of the plan!"

Hercules exaggerated a scowl. "Iolaus. You're starting to sound like Titus."

Iolaus looked close to exploding.

"Relax," Hercules told him, and waved at the guards, who ran into the corridor, stopped, gaped, and by their expressions couldn't figure out what to do next. A few words from Hercules told them all they needed to know; by the time Iolaus had recovered his composure, the rebels were trussed and ranged against the wall.

"Hercules."

He looked up; it was Jocasta.

"They're ready," she said, glancing at the scene as if she were used to seeing the results of a brawl. Then she spotted Rotus and walked over to him, gathering her shawl around her as if it were armor. "You murdered Jax," she said.

Rotus sneered. "He was a traitor, just like you."

Hercules and Iolaus saw her face at the same time, exchanged glances that suggested they probably didn't want to know what was going to happen next, and backed away toward the exit just as Titus stepped in.

"What . . . ?" Flustered and confused, he looked from his wife to the fallen rebels to Hercules and back to his wife. "Oh, my."

"It's over," Hercules told him. "The rebellion is over."

The councillor blinked several times. "They would have tried to . . . ?" He pointed at his chest.

"Yes."

"Oh, my."

"Don't get too confident, sir," Iolaus said then. "This is only the beginning."

20

Once the guards had been given their instructions, Hercules and the others returned to the porch. Jocasta immediately went to the guests, to assure them nothing was wrong, just a small problem.

Hercules held Titus back with a touch. "We know about Cire," he said, barely moving his lips, smiling at those who had turned to stare.

"Ah." Titus clasped his hands at his waist and nodded. "Ah."

"I don't understand. Why take a bribe?"

Titus' smile was brief and rueful. "There is no pension for a tyrant, Hercules. Our house here isn't ours; everything is paid for by the city." He shrugged. "Entirely my fault. When I realized this was the last time, I took a look at what we had, and what we didn't have, and . . ." He spread his hands. "I panicked."

"Herc," Iolaus said anxiously, halfheartedly waving to an impatient Venitia. "We don't have much time."

"The plan," Titus said.

Hercules nodded. "Tell your captain not to be too anxious when he sees what's about to happen. We'll take care of it."

"Unless he falls off," Iolaus said sourly.

Titus frowned. "The captain?"

Hercules sighed. "Look, just do it, Titus. The less you know, the better it will be. And whatever you do," he added, "do *not* pick a new queen."

Titus opened his mouth. He closed his mouth. He gathered his robes about him and, with a sickly smile, said, "I'm confused, but I'm in charge." And strode away.

Iolaus rubbed his cheek thoughtfully. "Did he say what I thought he said?"

"He did."

"We're doomed, Herc. We're doomed."

There was, however, no time for debate.

Titus herded summer queen contestants away from their table and lined them up along the top of the first step, facing the plaza. The crowd screamed and cheered, banging drums and tooting horns for their favorites. Then he beckoned Iolaus and Hercules to his side. The crowd screamed and cheered, banging drums and tooting horns and waving ribbons and streamers. Slipping easily into the role, Iolaus waved both arms and grinned while the crowd screamed and cheered and tooted horns and banged drums, and Hercules felt the beginning of a monumental headache.

He also saw the storm clouds.

They were darker.

And closer.

As Iolaus studied each woman, one hand behind his back, the other stroking his chin, Hercules looked to the head of the boulevard. The small group of people there were tooting and cheering just as robustly as those in the stands, but he could see the empty street behind them.

He could see the approaching horseman.

Glancing skyward, he silently offered a simple prayer for forgiveness from Demeter and Poseidon.

The breeze grew stronger, and he swept a hand over his face to keep the hair from his eyes. At the same time he caught Iolaus' eye with a stern look that told him to hurry it up, this wasn't the only task they had to perform tonight.

Iolaus nodded almost imperceptibly and stood with his back to the crowd, facing the nervous women.

He smiled at them all.

He smiled at the redhead in front of him, although the smile faltered somewhat when he saw the redhead standing next to the redhead in front of him.

Twins? Hercules thought; nobody told us there were twins.

He shifted over to Iolaus.

"Well," Iolaus said. "Will you look at this?"

"Lovely," Hercules answered, making a show for the crowd of being unable to make up his mind. Which he couldn't. Because neither of the redheads gave a sign to let him know which was which. Cire, apparently, had strong doubts about the plan.

Then the redhead on the left muttered, "By the

gods, will you hurry up, it's freezing out here.''

Iolaus grinned, and held out his hand to the redhead on the right.

Cire gasped and almost took a step back, until Hercules said, "Congratulations, you'll be fine."

She didn't move for several seconds.

"Damn," Sana muttered. "I knew I should have worn the one without the top."

Iolaus sputtered, but his hand remained steady.

Finally, doubtfully, Cire took it.

The plaza exploded in a frenzy of cheers and screams, the guests rose to their feet and applauded, trumpets were sounded from the roof of the council building, the women who hadn't been chosen were discreetly eased away by several acolytes, and Titus stepped forward to place an exquisitely wrought gold-leaf crown on Cire's head.

Hercules hadn't thought the noise could get any louder.

It did.

Then Iolaus, murmuring assurances to an obviously terrified Cire, led her grandly down the steps and across the tiles to the shrine in the plaza's center.

Hercules, with a reminding look at Titus, followed more slowly, amazed at the exuberant greeting the Themonians gave their new summer queen. He hadn't taken more than a few steps before he was nearly blinded by a blizzard of flowers and blossoms thrown by nearly everyone in the crowd.

All right, he thought as he stopped halfway down; now Holix, where are—

He was distracted by a commotion at the plaza's

south end, and did his best not to betray his great relief when a huge white horse forced its way through the gathering there and galloped across the ground. On its back rode a man swathed in black from head to boot, one hand on the animal's reins, the other waving wildly over his head.

The crowd was stunned into astonished silence.

He charged the shrine just as Iolaus moved to help Cire climb onto it.

Iolaus backed away fearfully.

The rider swung around the shrine and with his free arm scooped Cire onto his mount in front of him.

Wonderful, Hercules thought even as he raced down the steps; just keep going, boy, just keep going. And, he added when he saw the guards sweeping belatedly down the steps behind him, hurry it up, you idiot.

Holix did.

He completed his taunting circuit of the shrine, shouted something incomprehensible, and charged for the boulevard, Cire clinging desperately to the horse's mane.

"Beautiful," Hercules said as he came up beside Iolaus. "Beautiful."

Iolaus, doing a great job of looking as if he'd just been highly and expertly insulted, agreed. "As long as he makes it."

"He will."

They raced around the shrine as if attempting to catch the outlaw rider, and stopped when the horse did.

Holix shouted something again.

The horse reared and kicked out its forelegs.

It was an impressive sight.

Until Holix fell off.

No one in the plaza moved.

Except the pursuing guards, who swarmed across the tiles, armor clanking and leather creaking and red plumes bobbing, and surrounded Holix before he could get to his feet. Two grabbed the horse, and one gently eased Cire off the animal's back. By this time the audience had regained its senses and had begun to surge out of the stands and from their places behind the roping. Their intent was clear—take the rider from the guards and make sure he was never able to ride again by the simple expediency of removing his limbs, one joint at a time.

Suddenly Iolaus found himself having to maneuver the guards, and those reinforcements who quickly joined them, into a large circle to hold the maddened Themonians back. Hercules, meanwhile, hurried over to Holix and stood over him.

Holix smiled sheepishly. "I think I broke another rib."

Hercules knelt beside him and kept his voice low. "You were supposed to tie yourself on."

"But they'd see it," the young man protested in a whisper.

"You fell off."

Holix grimaced in pain. "Yeah. I noticed."

There was nothing else Hercules could do. The temptation to grab Cire and ride off himself died as soon as Titus arrived, huffing, red-faced, and using an elaborate pantomime both to tell the cheering-turned-snarling crowd that all was under control, and also to let Hercules know that if this was the plan, he hadn't a clue about what was going on.

Neither did Hercules.

By the time he was able to gather his wits about him and smack them a few times for coming up with this stupid plan in the first place, Titus had convinced most of the populace that this was, after all, only part of the show. Something new. Something exciting. When he was finished, the snarling had turned back to cheering, Cire had been put back on the thoroughly confused horse, and the judges were commanded to escort the summer queen to her holy site of contemplation.

Along with a squad of guards.

Before they left, however, the councillor took Hercules aside and said, "Explain."

That was the easy part.

If no one was at the site, Hercules said, the Klothon would come and then leave, doing no harm to anyone. All Hercules had to worry about then was Hera. And he had a plan for that.

Titus raised an all-too-expressive eyebrow. "Another plan?"

Hercules spread his arms. "What can I say? The guy fell off the horse."

"I saw that. Very well done. Most men would have killed themselves, landing like that. I must congratulate him." Titus frowned. "I've seen the clouds, Hercules. May I assume that's Hera at work? And that she may be at work a little sooner than you had"—he almost choked—"planned?"

Hercules could do nothing but nod unhappily.

Titus glared, was about to say something, but instead ordered the small procession on its way. The cheers began anew and the flowers and blossoms flew while Titus stayed Hercules with a look. That they were surrounded by dancing, celebrating people only made them more isolated.

"That storm," Titus said angrily. "It's going to destroy my city, isn't it?" A whip-shake of his head kept Hercules from responding. "I'm no hero, Hercules. The gods know that. I've done things I'm not proud of. But I love this city, and I love its people."

"Titus—" Hercules protested.

"No. Not a word. Not one word. Hera will get me for this, I'm sure, but . . ." He took a deep breath, and released it with a shudder. "The shrine. It's—"

Hercules grabbed his shoulder. "I know, Titus, I know. Iolaus found it this morning."

Suddenly the robes of office seemed much too large for his frame, and Titus much too old to rule. With all the gaiety around him, he looked like a man attending the funeral of a loved one.

And, Hercules realized, in a very real sense he was.

Titus walked away as the wind rose and the sky darkened. The torches and fire pans were lit as if on signal, filling the plaza with dancing light and racing shadows. Applause followed the leader, but he acknowledged none of it, turning only once, when he reached the fourth step and Jocasta met him.

Hercules saw them exchanging whispers, saw her lean into him and embrace him.

They were too small for the towering building above them.

Much too small.

He made no move to attract their attention. It wouldn't matter anyway. Yet he was afraid that Titus, facing disgrace and the destruction, would do something stupid.

What had to be done, then, had to be done swiftly.

He turned and pushed his way through the thinning crowd, each step a spark that tried to ignite his anger. At Hera, for bringing an essentially good man down to this level, and at himself for trying to be too clever.

When his anger finally flared, he began to run.

The Klothon was waiting, out there in the sea.

Before the night and the storm were over, one of them would be dead.

21

The storm didn't simply break.

It erupted.

The winds were hordes of banshees, shrieking through every alley and street, ripping banners to shreds, slamming shutters so hard they shattered if they weren't fastened quickly enough, spinning sandpaper dervishes of grit and garbage into the eyes of those who raced for shelter.

Once confined to the depths of the clouds, lightning broke free and spat over the city, and the thunder that followed shook the ground and hammered the buildings and made more than one man cry out in pain and fear.

What little light remained was a sickly, ominous black green.

Astounded that Iolaus could have gotten so far ahead of him, Hercules sprinted down the nearly deserted boulevard. He made no attempt to retrace the shortcut Venitia had shown them that morning; that was an easy invitation to getting hopelessly lost. Instead he kept to the center of the street, slowed by the wind slamming into his face, shoving at him from all sides, once slapping him square in the back and nearly toppling him into a chariot smashed against a shop wall.

When he finally reached the city's edge, he ran a hundred yards more and veered to his left, easily climbing the low grassless embankment that now rose above the boulevard on both sides.

Once he was separated from the buildings, there was no protection at all.

He ran, but the storm wouldn't permit a pace much faster than a brisk walk; lightning speared the ground behind him as if it were seeking him out; and at last the rain began, cold and hard, blinding him instantly, forcing him to raise an arm over his brow so that he could make his way without tripping and breaking a leg.

To the right the sea thundered, and the wind-driven spray blended with the rain.

A quick glance during a lightning flare nearly caused him to stop—waves twice and three times the height of a man arced over the beach, but crashed far beyond it.

The tide was in.

He knew it wouldn't be long before the sea reached the city. Had Themon remained in its original site, it wouldn't have lasted a hour; now it would be lucky to last the night.

The land rose, earth churned to mud, the grass grew slick.

Hercules struggled up the east side of the slope, half the time bent over so far he had to use his hands to pull himself along.

If we get out of this . . . he thought grimly.

When we get out of this, he corrected, none too optimistically, I am going to have a long talk with Iolaus. A real long talk. And if he says one word, I'm gonna deck him.

He fell only once, but in doing so slid a good ten feet back, cursing the entire way. When he regained his feet, using his hands to wipe the mud from his face, he ordered himself to slow down, because he would only wear himself out, and what good would he be then?

A blue-white bolt slammed into the flatland below.

On the other hand, he decided, deliberation was making him too easy a target.

He ran.

Rather, he tried to run, battling his own weariness as well as the storm's power, grinning mirthlessly when he reached the top. Swaying. Panting. Blinking away the salty rain as he looked around for the others.

He didn't locate them until a triple-forked bolt ripped through the clouds. They were near the cliff's edge, Iolaus flapping his arms helplessly as three guards grappled with Cire, and three others struggled with a length of thick rope the wind kept trying to wind around their necks.

An honor, huh? Hercules thought as he ran forward; the queen faces her destiny proudly, does she?

"Herc!" Iolaus yelled when he saw him. "Herc, they won't listen!"

Cire just glared over a guard's shoulder and screamed in his ear. The guard flinched, but held onto the rope.

It took only a second and Iolaus pointing angrily to locate the man in charge. Hercules grabbed his arm and spun him around. "Let her go!"

"Are you nuts?" the man answered, his lips blue with the cold. Nervously he drew a short sword from its scabbard. "They'll kill me!"

"They'll have to get through me first."

The guard glanced uneasily from side to side, torn between self-preservation and the duty he had been given.

"Herc!" Iolaus called.

"Come on, man," Hercules commanded the guard. "We haven't got all night."

"Herc!" Iolaus called, but Hercules still ignored him.

Just then Cire screamed again, lashing out with her feet, biting at whatever flesh or armor came near her teeth.

A wave exploded against the cliff, shaking the ground, spray and foam sweeping over the top to add to the downpour.

Finally the guard, nearly weeping, shook his head. "My duty, Hercules, my duty."

Hercules felt for the man, but right now he couldn't be bothered with duty or orders. He drew his arm back to slap the guard aside, and swore when the trio with the rope barreled into him and their leader, dropping the rope as they stumbled as fast as they could toward the trees.

The guard bellowed at his men.

"Herc, will you please listen to me!" Iolaus shouted.

That was when Hercules finally saw it.

It rose through the strobe of the lightning. Slowly.

The shadow in his dream.

He saw the horns first, thick and dark, aiming forward from either side of a head bisected by a bony ridge that began between its eyes and disappeared behind the crown of its head.

The eyes themselves were vivid green and slanted upward at the corners. Nothing in them but the reflection of the storm.

Once alerted to the danger, the guards bolted, leaving Cire on the ground to crawl inland as fast as she could. Hercules ran to stand over her, Iolaus at his side.

They were less than ten feet from the edge of the cliff.

The monstrous head cleared the top, steady in the howling wind.

Below the eyes, the head was long and narrow, resembling a serpent but with lips that curled back to expose a quartet of fangs half as large as a man, one pair on top, the other on the bottom.

Iolaus had his sword out.

Hercules met the Klothon's gaze and held it, seeing in the next series of flashes the diamond-shape scales that covered the head and part of a long thin neck. The scales glittered like crystal prisms.

The thing was, at the same time, both beautiful and horrid.

And in every flash of lightning, Hercules could feel the weight of its shadow.

And the weight of Hera's fury and lust for revenge.

"Don't move," Hercules said, and realized that he couldn't move even if he wanted to, because Cire had grabbed his left leg and was clinging like a sprung bear trap.

"Cire," he whispered fiercely, *"let go."*

"Are you nuts?" was her reply. "I'm this thing's dinner!"

He stared at the Klothon's eyes. "I can't move with you hanging on down there."

"You just said not to move," Cire told him with maddening stubbornness.

Iolaus shifted to his right. One step. Two, before the creature swiveled its head to follow his hesitant progress. Iolaus froze.

Another huge wave struck the cliff, and the Klothon jerked back, tilting its head toward the clouds and roaring at the storm.

Hercules couldn't help noticing all the teeth in its gaping maw. The kind meant for rending, not for chewing.

He also saw the band of comparatively pale, ribbed flesh Poseidon had told him about; it seemed to run from the throat down as much of the neck as he could see.

Swell; all he had to do was get in there without the beast knowing, and slice it down about, oh, ten, fifteen feet.

He looked at his swordless hands.

"Damn."

Iolaus sidestepped again, just as another wave struck the beast and the cliff. And again the Klothon reared, swinging its head ponderously from side to side, leaning forward, leaning back.

Hercules almost smiled.

"Cire, let go," he said tightly.

Finally, she complied, but she didn't flee; instead she curled into a tight ball and looked up at Hercules in terror.

He signaled Iolaus to move again at the next wave. When Iolaus did so, Hercules lunged toward the cliff edge and looked down.

This time he did grin.

Although much of the Klothon was still submerged in water, he saw two massive feet gripping the cliff face. Or trying to. Its black claws had a difficult time gaining purchase on the storm-slick rocks, nearly losing their hold each time a wave thundered past the boulders to strike the creature's shoulders and the base of its neck.

Iolaus shouted.

Hercules leaped back and to the left, feeling the sweep of the great head over the spot where he'd just been. As he scrambled frantically to his feet he nearly lost his balance; seeing the gouge where the upper fangs had hit the earth instead of him made his legs want to take charge and leave, with or without the rest of him.

The Klothon dipped its head a second time, aiming for Iolaus, who dodged neatly, and from one knee was able to nick the side of its jaw with a desperate sweep of his sword.

It reared, bellowed, shook its head angrily, and almost toppled in the tide- and storm-driven rush of the next huge wave.

Another attempt by the Klothon, and Hercules easily got out of its way. That didn't really surprise him—the Klothon was a creature of the sea, and while its size and weight were easily borne by the water, here on land they were an incumbrance.

"Iolaus," he called as the beast fought for a grip after another wave. "Iolaus, get him to come to you."

Iolaus gaped. "Do . . . what?"

The Klothon roared.

Frantically Hercules signaled, ending with a *trust me* that, from Iolaus's expression, probably wasn't all that persuasive.

Still, he had to test something, and this was the only way.

He braced himself.

And waited.

Iolaus shrugged, yelled something about his funeral, then turned to the recovering Klothon and waved his arms, danced, ran to the edge of the cliff and back, stuck out his tongue, and seemed to be considering throwing a rock or two, when the monster pulled back its head, measured the distance, and lashed out.

Iolaus yelped and threw himself to the ground, covering his head with his arms.

Without hesitating, Hercules leaped toward the Klothon's head as it completed its sweeping motion, and grabbed the nearest horn, pulling as hard as he could as the Klothon rose.

The head lowered, twisting to one side, in the direction of the pull.

Hercules was dragged several feet before he released the horn, yelled to Iolaus, and ran for the trees. On the way, he snatched Cire under one arm and ignored her cries of protest until they were safe.

"You're crazy!" she yelled, slapping harmlessly at his chest.

Iolaus, his front slick with mud, only looked toward the sea, brow creased in thought.

"It's the only way," Hercules told him.

"No, it's not," Cire said. "We just keep running, that's all."

In the flashes of lightning they could see the green eyes of the Klothon searching for its prey, could sense the strain as it tried to drag itself higher.

"I don't get it," Iolaus said. "Why doesn't it come up?"

Cire put a fist to her chin and pulled her lower lip between her teeth. "The waves," she said through chattering teeth. "I saw it before. They hit it, and they drag it back, too. If it wasn't for the storm, it . . ." She looked at them both. "Wait a minute. Wait a minute, Hercules, you can't be thinking that—"

She didn't finish.

One chance, he told his friend. There's only one chance, and if Poseidon's right, we may be okay; if he's wrong, we're going to have dinner with Hades tonight. All you have to do is follow my lead.

Iolaus shoved his hands back through his hair.

"You know, all this talk about my funeral was only a joke."

Hercules smiled, winked, and turned to Cire to explain her part.

She balked.

"It's the weight we need," he said earnestly, "and you haven't got it."

Cire remained unconvinced. "If that's supposed to be a compliment, it's a little late, don't you think?"

The Klothon bellowed.

The storm intensified, and they looked back at the city, at the lightning strikes that lifted bright smoke over the rooftops.

At last Cire swallowed and said, "I'm not a hero."

"Someone else told me that today," Hercules said gently. "He was wrong, too."

Iolaus was tired of waiting. He said, "Go," and headed for the cliff.

Where the Klothon waited, watching every step.

22

Hercules did his best to ignore the rage of the storm, concentrating on the Klothon and its pursuit, its head swaying slowly, jerking only when a wave threatened to unbalance it.

It knows, he thought, and shook the thought off.

"Herc?" Iolaus tried futilely to dry his hands on his vest. "What are the odds?"

"Thinking about the odds will get you killed. Just think about what we have to do."

Cire walked half a hundred yards to their left, her head bowed against the wind and rain, her hands pressed tightly to her thighs.

She didn't look up until the Klothon showed its fangs and roared.

"I hate your plans," Iolaus confessed with a rueful laugh.

Hercules didn't reply.

He watched Cire, willing her not to panic, afraid that even if she didn't, she wouldn't be fast enough to get away.

The Klothon struck at her before she was in range.

She didn't jump, or run away.

Iolaus sighed loudly enough for both of them.

"Watch," Hercules told him. "Watch it, the way it moves."

The Klothon struck at Cire again, but not as a snake would. The head came down in a long rapid arc, as if the creature knew enough to use its weight to give it speed. Swift enough to catch the unwary, almost swift enough to catch even the wary.

The sea's support again, Hercules supposed. If he was right, they had a chance.

Cire stopped and looked over at the men.

Iolaus waved, and Hercules nodded.

This time the Klothon struck at them, too close, and they leaped to avoid the sharp fangs.

They moved closer. Warily. Listening to the sea match the Klothon's roars.

"At least there's the lightning," Iolaus said, bracing himself.

Just then the lightning stopped.

Nothing left but the night. And the storm.

"Nice," said Hercules.

"It's a gift," Iolaus answered gloomily.

It was bad enough being blinded by the night; what was worse, the Klothon had stopped roaring, and all they could hear was the sea hitting the cliff.

Hercules had to remind himself to breathe.

Suddenly a single lightning bolt sliced out of the clouds and struck the water.

In the brief illumination Hercules was able to dis-

201

cern the huge green eyes not ten feet from where he stood.

He yelped and threw himself backward, feeling the push of air as the snout missed him by inches, the nearest fang leaving behind a thin tracery of white.

"I am not happy," Iolaus told him from somewhere in the dark.

Iolaus couldn't get his hands dry.

He knew he'd need all the advantage he could get when he performed his part in this madness, but he couldn't get his hands dry enough.

Not that it would matter much if Hercules missed and he didn't. Or if he missed and Hercules didn't. Or if one of them slipped and was caught by those teeth.

He shuddered.

"Stop it," Hercules said, somewhere to his left.

"What do you mean?"

"Just stop it."

Iolaus scowled. He hated it when Herc did that; it was a reminder that sometimes the guy just wasn't human.

Still, he'd feel a whole lot better if he could just dry his hands.

Another bolt forked in several directions, lingering just long enough for Hercules to drop to his knees without thinking, and for him to see Cire run forward instead of back, the underside of the jaw brushing her spine and knocking her to the ground.

The beast was higher this time, he realized.
It had found purchase on the rocks.

The wind stopped.
The rain stopped.
Nothing left but the sea.

Hercules felt the tension, the gathering of a force as the Klothon prepared to launch its last attack.

Iolaus gripped his hand, squeezed once, hard, and let him go.

"One chance," he said. He swiped the hair from his eyes. "We need just one chance."

"Is that a prayer or a statement of fact?"

"Yes."

"That's what I was afraid of."

The storm's second eruption took them by surprise, beating them to their knees in a fury of rain and wave and wind. Hercules heard Iolaus curse, saw him then as the lightning renewed its assault on the city.

They stood and looked for Cire.

Hercules couldn't see her.

No, he thought; she wouldn't have.

"There," Iolaus said, pointing.

The white of her gown was an eerie glow at the edge of the cliff, her hair as bright as the unnatural lighting. Her arms were up, and he could see her lips moving as she taunted the Klothon, dared it to attack again.

He and Iolaus closed the distance between them, knowing this had to be the moment.

And when it happened, Hercules stopped thinking and simply let his strength take over.

It's all right, Iolaus told himself, bouncing on the balls of his feet, rolling his shoulders, frantically trying to convince himself he was ready for anything; it's going to be all right.

He had long since abandoned the notion of attempting to change Hercules' mind. If there were other arguments, he couldn't think of any; if Cire was ready, then he had to be ready as well.

Still, Venitia and her squeaking were looking awfully good about now.

But when it happened, Venitia was forgotten, and so were all his fears.

This was war; there was nothing left to do but fight.

The wave sprayed over the edge just as the Klothon swung at Cire from her left. She waited until the last moment, to be sure it wouldn't stop, then lunged for the edge, arms outstretched.

The Klothon had jerked as the wave struck him, and in so doing had missed her.

At least Hercules thought it had, but he was already off his feet, reaching desperately for the right-hand horn, grabbing it and nearly losing it as it swung past him, clenching his jaw as he held it, and *pulled,* feeling but not seeing Iolaus do the same.

It happened too slowly, and much too swiftly.

He saw the huge eye, staring at him, hating him.

He felt his grip begin to slip, and only then remembered the rope the guards had left behind.

The head kept its arc, twisting to one side, then the other, bringing them over the edge.

Hanging there.

Hanging.

The eye didn't blink as Hercules strained, drawing on the power that was his father's legacy.

Hanging for what seemed like a lifetime, and much longer.

Until Hercules' strength, and the sudden added weight, brought the monstrous head down.

Hard and fast.

The tallest boulder caught it just below the throat, and there was a moment's resistance before he heard the flesh part and the Klothon begin to scream.

The next thing Hercules knew he was flying. Tumbling toward the beach that boiled with the last wave.

He thought he heard Iolaus yelling, knew he heard the Klothon bellowing in agony, just before something struck his head and everything merged with the storm and night.

Iolaus fell, thought he heard Hercules, knew he heard the Klothon, but the idea of landing on the beach made him twist in midair and watch the wave recede just as he reached it. The water wasn't deep, but it was, thank the gods, deep enough to slow him down when he hit the sand with palms out to brace himself.

A push, another twist, and he was on his hands and knees as the water swirled away, sucked into the base of another wave somewhere out there.

When he could stand he began to run. He didn't bother to look for Hercules; there was something else he had to do first. Before the next wave came in and smashed him against the rocks.

Stumbling, for the first time grateful for the lighting that kept him from colliding with the high boulders, he made his way along the base of the cliff, pushing at every rock until suddenly there weren't any rocks left.

He saw the wave as he fell into the tunnel.

Boy, that sucker's big, was the only thing he could think as he pushed into a run that had him halfway down the dark tunnel before the walls shook, water surged around his knees, and he realized that for some reason, the wave couldn't follow.

Five minutes later he saw the glow.

Five minutes after that he was back outside, grinning broadly and wishing someone was there to see him.

That's when he saw the wave cresting cliff-high over his head.

Big, he thought, and closed his eyes, and waited.

23

A voice tried to convince Hercules to open his eyes, but he didn't want to. It was nice in here. No monsters, no vengeful goddesses, no storms, no women with squeaky voices. Nice. And until that gentle nagging began, quiet.

"Go away," he muttered.

The voice kept on.

"Leave me alone. I think I'm dead, and I think I like it."

Laughter now. Familiar laughter, and against his better judgment, Hercules opened his eyes.

He lay on his back on an expanse of grass and sand. The clouds were gone, the sun flirting with the western horizon. Seagulls and shore birds swarmed over the beach, picking at the debris the waves had left behind. The breeze was slow and warm.

His head hurt.

He groaned and sat up, touching the lump at the back of his skull and hissing.

"Sorry about that."

A man sat to his left, grinning smugly.

It took a moment for Hercules to remember what had happened. Then he looked sharply to his right, holding his breath until he spotted Iolaus, lying peacefully on his back a few yards away.

"He's out," Poseidon said. "I thought it would be best for a while."

"Is he . . . ?"

"A little battered, a lot bruised. A brave man, Nephew. He destroyed Hera's shrine, and that took care of the storm." A finger poked his arm. "You, on the other hand, have a lot to learn about sea monsters."

"Tell me about it," Hercules said, the ache in his head competing now with the ache in all his muscles. Far beyond where Iolaus lay—a mile, not much less—he saw the toothlike rocks.

Even at this distance he could tell the Klothon was no longer there.

He was halfway to his feet before Poseidon took his arm and pulled him down.

"I tidied up a little," the sea god explained. "Except for the head. I left the head. Otherwise, they'd never know what happened."

Hercules saw people then. The glint of waning sunlight on brass armor and spears.

"You want something to eat?"

"What?" Hercules saw two thick slices of bread in his uncle's hand, and something red and dripping between them. "What's that?"

Poseidon smiled and shrugged. "Steak."

"What's that?"

"What you get from the flank of a dead critter, what else?" The sea god waved the fillet-of-sea-monster sandwich. "You want some?"

Hercules shuddered. "No, thanks, I'll pass." He looked around again. "Cire. Where's—"

"Asleep under the trees," Poseidon answered patiently. "You don't think I'd forget her, do you? Most courageous woman I've ever met."

Hercules' eyes widened. "You talked to her?"

"She'll think it's a dream."

"It *was* a dream. A nightmare. I—" He stopped and very slowly turned toward his uncle. "It was you, wasn't it?"

Poseidon stood and brushed the sand from his legs. "Me?" he said, so innocently that Hercules had to laugh. "Don't know what you're talking about."

As Iolaus began to stir, Hercules and Poseidon walked down to the water.

"You held it back," Hercules said, thinking aloud, remembering. "It would have made it up the cliff, but you held it back."

Poseidon kept walking.

"Then you caught me." Gingerly he touched his head. "What did I hit?"

Poseidon waved his trident and lifted a shoulder in apology.

"She'll be mad, you know," Hercules said, louder now that Poseidon was in the sea to his waist. "She'll hate you for this."

Poseidon turned and walked backward. "She never liked me anyway, Hercules. And she'll be madder at you for escaping again than she ever will be at me."

"Uncle . . ." He didn't know what to say except a humble "Thank you."

Poseidon waved the sandwich as he sank below the waves. "Don't mention it. The tuna, by the way, will love you. Klothon's going to last me for a long, long time."

He laughed heartily and vanished, and a huge wave rose from the spot where he'd stood, crested, and carried Hercules a good twenty yards toward the grass.

When he sat up sputtering and spitting, he heard, "Sorry again, Nephew," and another delighted laugh.

Hercules didn't bother to stand up. He drew up his knees and stared at the water, letting the last of the warm sun dry him.

"That was Poseidon, wasn't it?"

He nodded as Iolaus dropped down beside him.

"I thought he was a wave." Iolaus frowned, then shrugged. "Funny, I thought he was a lot bigger, too."

"Oh, he is," Hercules said fondly. "You have no idea how really big he is."

They walked back to Themon in twilight.

The city was battered, but still standing more or less intact. Walls had cracked, roofs had caved in, and the sea had indeed swept up the boulevard all the way to the plaza. But there was nothing that couldn't be repaired with hard work and time.

A few questions of passersby brought them to the house of Titus Perical, where an awestruck servant let them in. When Jocasta saw who had arrived, she wept with joy and hugged them, blessed them, wept, hugged them, and finally said, "The stories are true."

"The Klothon?" Iolaus said. "Well, maybe they—"

She grinned. "No. About you two."

Once more, Hercules was embarrassed, and tried to cover it by asking about Titus. Jocasta wiped her eyes with the backs of her hands and led them to a room near the back. Titus lay on a bed, covered to his chin, his hands at his sides, trembling.

"He was out there the whole time," Jocasta told them, her voice filled with anger and love. "Directing everything. The fool. He said Hera's curse would get him anyway, so . . ."

Hercules knelt beside the old man and laid a hand on his. The man was pale, too pale, and his breathing sounded like the rasp of rough metal.

Titus opened his eyes.

Hercules smiled.

"Did we win?" the old man asked weakly.

"We won." Hercules squeezed the hand gently. "Thanks to you."

Titus tried to laugh, ended up coughing instead. "It was all my fault. Pride, Hercules, and a dose of self-importance, can make you do very foolish things."

Hercules shook his head. "It was Hera from the beginning; you couldn't have fought her. You did what you thought was right." He paused and, at Iolaus' nod, added, "And you did well."

Titus closed his eyes. "Too late."

"No. You'll be fine."

Titus opened one eye. "I . . . I suppose you have inside information?" he asked wearily.

Hercules couldn't help a quiet laugh. "You could say that. Yes."

He waited until he thought the old man had fallen asleep, then touched his shoulder with a finger and headed for the door.

"Demeter," Titus wheezed suddenly, "is going to be really pissed, isn't she?"

"Maybe," Hercules agreed. "But Hera's not too happy either. Demeter I can talk to, if she doesn't know what happened already. Hera?" He shrugged, and when Titus didn't respond, he left, following Jocasta down a short hall at her insistence.

In another room he found Holix and Cire.

"They're going to stay with us," Jocasta explained in a whisper. "They'll have their own cottage, I think. Holix claims he knows something about horses."

"Yeah, right," Iolaus said good-naturedly. "Everything except how to stay on one."

Hercules laughed.

Holix laughed.

Cire jumped to her feet.

"What's the matter?" Holix asked, inhaling sharply when one of his broken ribs reminded him it was broken.

"I can't find my knife!" Cire cried.

Iolaus backed off, pulling Hercules with him. They still laughed, but they weren't taking any chances.

At the front door, Jocasta thanked them again, so fervently that Hercules felt a blush rise to his face. He kissed her cheek and said, yes, they would both be honored to visit the new place once Titus was well.

"I'll miss you. Miss you both."

She kissed their cheeks and hurried away.

Iolaus cleared his throat, clapped once, and said, "Okay. That's it. We're done. Let's get something to eat and hit the road."

"Iolaus, it's almost dark."

Iolaus stood in front of him, reached up to put his hands on Hercules' shoulders, and stared him in the eye. "Tell me the truth: do you want to spend one more hour in this place than you absolutely have to?"

"But I thought you were a hero," Hercules said mildly. "All those women just waiting to hear your stories . . . are you sure you want to pass that up?"

"Herc, what I want—"

A voice from inside the Perical house called his name. Sweetly. Insistently. With a definite squeak.

"Meet you on the road," Iolaus said, and was gone.

A moment later Venitia raced by, raced back, said, "Are you sure he's not married?"—and raced away.

Once he had stopped laughing, Hercules took to the street. No hurry. Nothing to do but get back on the road.

All in all, it hadn't been that bad.

A monster was dead, a city spared . . . an old man saved in more ways than one.

Best of all, Hera had been thwarted again.

And he had survived.

It was that time of day, and as he passed people

cleaning up, gossiping, a few still eating their last meal, he decided that perhaps it was time for him as well.

Time to go home and finally finish that wall.

JURASSIC PARK™
THE RIDE

YOU'LL WISH IT WAS JUST A MOVIE.

COMING SUMMER '96